M000202200

hope
as wide
as a prairie sky

a story of courage and grace

hope
as wide as a prairie sky

a story of courage and grace

Linda Whitesitt

Copyright © 2019 Linda Whitesitt

All rights reserved. No part of this publication may be reproduced, transmitted, scanned, distributed, stored in any form or by any means, electronic, mechanical, photocopying, recording, or otherwise, without prior written permission from the author.

My grateful acknowledgment to the following online publication where "Striking Water from a Rock" (in a different form) first appeared: Blue Heron Review (Issue 11, Winter 2019).

This book is the memoir the author imagines her grandmother would have written. Based on family stories, memorabilia and historical resources, it reflects the author's best understanding of how her grandmother would have described her life. Several events, along with some of the letters and most of the dialogue, have been invented by the author. The reader should consider this book a literary improvisation on the author's grandmother's life and not a work of nonfiction.

Cover photograph (author's grandparents' homestead in eastern Montana) © Linda Whitesitt; author photo by Bennett Lentczner

Published 2019 by prairie vision press (Charlotte, NC)
Printed in the United States of America

ISBN: 978-0-578-56658-0
Library of Congress Control Number: 2019913264

for Bennett
forever

. . . we are saved by hope . . .

—Romans 8:24

Contents

A Future Bigger Than Hope Can See

God Stood Weeping at Our Side

When Just Living is a Miracle

A Love Never to be Undone

My Swedish Roots

My maternal grandparents:

Hulda Egedia Peterson, called **Gedia** (1878–1963)
  born in Alexandria, Minnesota

Gustaf Elof Jonsson [Johnson in the U.S.], called **Elof**
  (1865–1945)
  born in Hässleby, Jönköping, Sweden

Elof's parents:

Kristina Karolina Johansdotter (1833–1913)
  born in Hässleby, Jönköping, Sweden

Johannes Peter Jonsson (1826–1894)
  born in Hässleby, Jönköping, Sweden

Gedia's parents:

Johanna Eliasdotter (1837–1914)
   born in Ljur, Älvsborg Lan, Sweden

Anders Petter Petterson (1835–1910)
   born in Ornunga, Älvsborg Lan, Sweden

Gedia's grandparents:

Maternal:

Christina Svensdotter (1816–1838)
   Christina died when Johanna was two.
   Her father then married Christina's sister,
   Johanna Svensdotter (1818–1906);
   both born in Ljur, Skattegården, Sweden

Elias Bengtsson (1808–1891)
   born in Horla, Älvsborg Lan, Sweden

Paternal:

Ingeborg Jonsdotter (1803–1889)
   born in Vaselid, Östergården, Sweden

Petter Pehrson (1796–1874)
   born in Vaselid, Östergården, Sweden

Preface

I have prairie dust in my bones—dirt from the sod my Swedish great-grandparents broke on the tallgrass prairie of Minnesota; traces of soil their youngest daughter, Gedia, and her Swedish husband, Elof, tilled on the Saskatchewan plains; bits and pieces from the plowed earth of their second homestead on the shortgrass prairie of eastern Montana—every speck as much a part of me as the stories Gedia tells in this book.

Born Hulda Egedia Peterson, my grandma Gedia (pronounced Gid-ja) came to live with her daughter and son-in-law (Judith and Donald, my parents) shortly before I was born. It would be her job to take care of me while they worked, her labor of love to feed me and change me, play with me and potty train me, read to me and teach me how to read. I am who I am because of my kind-hearted, steel-willed grandmother.

Today I'm almost as old as she was when she first held me in her arms, and I'd like to see her again; hear her strong, gravely voice tell me tales of her life on the prairie; have her introduce me to Gustaf Elof Johnson, the grandfather who died before I was born. What would she tell me about her parents' and grandparents' immigration to America? What tales would she share about how she fell in love with a man thirteen years her senior and decided to follow him in the great turn-of-the-century adventure of transforming grassland into the world's granary? How did she and Grandpa live through the deaths of their children?

Thinking there must be something left of their rugged, pioneering lives, I started to root around in my attic for remnants of who they were and what they did, gleaned box after box for any shred of family history. In a large plastic bin, I found a shoebox from JCPenney's department store labeled "Daddy's things," recognized the writing as my mother's. Seeing the curve of her letters was a treasure all its own. Inside, I picked out Elof's love poems to Gedia; his small, red-velvet autograph book filled with greetings from his first American friends; a few letters and documents; a couple of photographs; his diary, in Swedish, from his last years; his funeral album; an old Baptist hymn book. Stacked around the shoebox were letters Grandma wrote to my mom during the second World War, Gedia's favorite book of poetry, my mother's high school diary, the journal of family stories she started to write a few years before her death, and an envelope marked in Mom's hand—"Linda, you will want this. Aunt Minnie's story about their Swedish parents." Grandma's sister! What a delicious discovery!

Returning to the JCPenney box, I picked up in my hands what Grandpa had touched with his own. "You have his thumbs," Mother used to tell me as she outlined mine with her finger. "Even when you were a baby, I could tell they were the same." Perhaps, I thought, Grandpa and I share the same memories as well.

I turned to the Internet, scoured it for information not only about Grandma and Grandpa, but also their prairie friends, the ones they knew in Minnesota who went with them to Canada and then to Montana, and Grandma's brother Edward who, with his family, accompanied Gedia and Elof on their homesteading moves. Slowly, click by click, I uncovered information about my grandparents tucked away in local histories, and most astonishing of all, I found Edward's grandson Jim Peterson, who shared family photos along with his meticulously researched book on our shared ancestors. Equally as fortuitous, I stumbled on the family in eastern Montana who bought the old homestead from Gedia and Elof. Now deceased, their son Dennis Pluhar still lives there, and he invited me to put a visit to "the old place" on my bucket list. He'd show me around. Tell me family stories.

I basked in what I'd found. Gathered the stories around me. Started to write. Stopped. Realized I would always want to know more. So I listened. Listened for Grandma Gedia, who always was eager to put in her two cents. Heard her say she'd like to tell me about my ancestors' pioneering lives in her own words. I paused, then I started to write again, this time in her voice, imagining myself inside her story.

Knowing her love of poetry, I chose to write in verse, and after many attempts at different forms, I decided couplets were the best fit for her book of memories. The white space reminded me of the emptiness of the prairie; the couplets, the intimacy of my grandparents' love and the furrows of dirt they spent their lives turning.

Hearing Gedia's "two cents" has filled me with awe for my grandparents, dreamers called "honyockers"—homesteaders chasing honey (land and opportunity). With hope as wide as a prairie sky, they chased land to grow a future on, then fought to keep going when the unthinkable threatened to tear their lives apart. As I've continued to gather information and sift through memorabilia, all the while trying to discern how Grandma would describe her life on the prairie, I've become filled with gratitude for all my prairie ancestors and the dust they've mingled in my bones. In searching for their lives, I've unearthed endless nourishment for my own.

After years of looking and listening, writing and rewriting, I've begun to share Gedia's story with others and in the process, I've noticed how hearing about her life has encouraged them to recall anecdotes from their own family history. It's as if her memories have triggered their own. Then, like me, they want answers to long-held questions about their ancestors' lives and wonder what information they might uncover on their own Internet treasure hunt. As I tell them about my adventures finding Gedia and Elof, they embrace the possibility that if I've been able to forge a link with grandparents who have been gone for more than half a century, then perhaps they can as well.

I coax them to start looking, tell them that perhaps they'll find stories related specifically to their forebears. If not, I'm certain they'll chance on bits and pieces of what their grandparents' lives must have been like in stories about other people's ancestors. They might even light on their own story. I suggest that as they take on their own pilgrimage of discovery, they'll learn, as I did, not to be surprised by the connections they come upon, relationships past and present that feed their soul. Finally, I urge them to take counsel in Frederick Buechner's reminder that "all our words are in the end one story, one vast story about being human, being together, being here."

* * *

And now for the story I think Gedia would have written, a story that begins and ends with words I imagine her addressing to me . . .

Dearest Linda

The other day I came across these words
in a faded copy of an old magazine:

> *It is all a battle, life [in the Canadian Northwest];*
> *but the battle makes for iron in the blood*
>
> *and iron in the will, and that*
> *is the spirit of the pioneer.*

I couldn't have said it better myself, and what's more,
we must've had a right good amount of that iron

to live through the troubles
the good Lord laid on our doorstep.

Remember when I'd take you to church
when you were little?

We'd be singing one of my favorite hymns,
and you'd tug my sleeve and say,

Grandma, do you have to sing so loud?
Everyone's looking.

Sure do, I'd say.
Gotta make sure the Lord hears me.

Well, the Lord heard me singing,
just like He heard me praying.

And you know what I was praying for?
Iron. Iron in my blood.

Iron to get me through the hard times.
Iron to keep in reserve during the good times.

It's time I told you why I sang so loud
and prayed so hard,

time you heard the story
of my life and how,

more often than not,
just living was a miracle.

I want you to learn about
the homesteaders who live

inside you; feel the strength
of your pioneer ancestors

who claimed land in the prairies
of Minnesota, Saskatchewan and Montana;

imagine the tiredness of sodbusters
who worked sun-up to sun-down

plowing and planting,
hoeing and harvesting.

You come from sturdy stock—
resilient people who buried children too early

and went hungry to feed their families,
immigrants who could have turned

their losses into bitterness,
but chose hope instead.

Your soul sings with the faith of people who prayed
not for a life without suffering, but for the strength

to prevail through the death and despair
they knew were coming.

Their stories, the stories passed down to me,
my story, your grandpa's stories,

your mama's stories,
all these stories stand within you

like the Russian nesting dolls
you played with as a child.

It seems like only yesterday
I sat watching you open

one doll after another, laughing
at how surprised you were

each time you found
a smaller doll hiding within.

These stories are like
those dolls.

Unstack them.
Read my words.

Find yourself
waiting inside.

When Land is a Stranger

An Act of Faith

To follow a plow is an act of faith,
an offering of hard work

in exchange for our lives,
all the while knowing the land—

and the sun and rain who feed her—
are capricious collaborators

filling our bellies in good times,
starving us in bad.

Tillers of the soil,
we lived in that risk.

And when, for lack of land,
we picked up our families,

moved them to places unknown,
we raised that risk, gambled

with lives only the desperate
have the courage to wager.

My husband, Elof, and I knew this.
Papa and Mama knew this.

And more than a decade before
I was born, Grandpa knew this.

It was in the winter of 1867
when he said to Grandma,

>   *Our children will never make*
>   *much headway here in Sweden.*
>
>   *But in America, if all of us*
>   *go together, we can claim*
>
>   *six homesteads—*
>   *nine hundred and sixty acres.*

All five of their children, some with families
of their own, would have to agree.*

Everyone was going,
or no one was.

Throughout the winter they weighed
whether they should leave or stay,

asked themselves if they could believe
a friend back from America

who told of a land rich in resources,
if they could trust railroad ads peddling

plentiful harvests and abundant opportunities.
At the same time, they remembered

their own meager stocks and
years of crop failures and famine.

As the days lengthened and the season
stretched into spring, they were certain

of one thing—they had no land left
to divide and pass on to their families.

Perhaps the only way to give
those they loved a future

was to carry to America the hope
that love for one's children demands.

*Gedia's entire extended family immigrated to America—
Elias and Johanna (Gedia's grandparents); Johanna and
Anders (her parents); their three small children, Johan Emil
(five), Selma Elisabeth (three) and Ida Charlotte (one); and
Johanna's (Gedia's mother's) half-siblings—Klara and her
husband, Frederick, with their three small children; Charlotte
(Lottie), engaged to Henrik Frantzick; Johannes and his wife,
Ella Maja; and Henrik, the youngest in the family.

Belonging to the Land

Mama was thirty, Papa, thirty-two, when
the families started to talk about leaving Sweden.

> *If we go to America,* they asked each other,
> *how will we part with the land that made us?*

Mama loved her Swedish land,
regarded it as a guardian of the memory

of her mother who had died
when Mama was only two.

She'd cared for it after her father remarried,
farmed her own tiny parcel when he divided

a portion of his land between her and her sister Klara
after their double wedding in 1860.

It was land she'd tilled and coaxed,
laid her body on when she grew tired.

Land where she'd planted her feet
when she cured meats and curdled milk,

sheared sheep and leached ashes for soap,
cut peat from bogs for heat.

Mama saw herself in her land, in the sun
and the moon and the rain who were her partners.

If we go to America, she wondered, *who will I be
in a land that knows me only as stranger?*

Papa grew up about a mile across the valley
from Mama on land his forebears

had worked for generations,
first as tenant farmers, then as owners.

Centuries of family stories had been etched
in its ground, witnessed by its trees.

Everywhere he looked, Papa could read
the history of his kin in the land.

Every breeze that brushed his face carried
their voices, their breath, their songs.

If we go to America, he wondered, *who will I be
in a land that doesn't remember their music?*

Forsaking Certainty

As much as Mama believed
leaving Sweden might shatter

who she was, as sad as Papa felt
about severing his roots,

they knew they had no choice
but to chase a future they couldn't see.

With the decision made,
there was much to get ready.

Mama made lists
of what to take—

copper kettles and teapots,
her favorite coffee grinder,

a well-used mortar and pestle,
steel forks and knives with horn handles,

blue-figured English Willow ware
(a wedding gift from Grandma and Grandpa),

feather pillows and ticks,
linens of every sort.

Expecting harsh winters, she wove
heavy material, sewed extra clothing,

spent days with her hands busy at work,
her mind brimming with worry.

When she finished, she piled everything
into new trunks her Anders had made,

tucking in bits and pieces of Sweden—
a leaf, a stone, a pressed flower—

keepsakes to help her hang onto
the home she was leaving.

With every blanket she folded,
every item she stuffed between pillows,

she couldn't help wonder whether
the hands grinding coffee, boiling water,

shaking out clothes on the other side
of the Atlantic would feel like her own.

A Mother's Good-bye

Standing on the crowded dock
in April 1868, waiting to board the ship

that would take her and her family
from Gothenburg, Sweden to Hull, England,

Mama watched as Papa's mother,
her back straight and shoulders set,

her eyes dry, said good-bye
to Papa and his brother:

> *We will never meet again*
> *on this side of the grave,*

> *but on the day of resurrection,*
> *we shall again be together.*

A mother.
Leaning against time.

A mother knowing there was only one thing
that would ease her emptiness—

her belief that one day
the good Shepherd would find

the sons she was losing
and bring them home again.

Navigating a Sky of Dreams

Standing on deck, holding their one-year-old daughter,
Ida Charlotte, in her arms, Mama leaned

against Papa as their ship, the "Peruvian,"
left Liverpool harbor.

Papa, carrying three-year-old Selma Elizabeth,
and squeezing the hand of Johan Emil, five,

widened his stance to steady himself,
offer his wife the support she needed.

Stranger to the sea, uncomfortable
with water's shifting surface,

Mama struggled to find her balance.
Seeing land turn to memory

untethered her from the woman
she knew herself to be. Disoriented

by the empty sweep of ocean and sky,
she fought to hold onto who she was.

Their journey was difficult.
Storms in the North Sea

threatened to turn
the ship on its side.

Another in the Atlantic broke Mama's arm.
Icebergs loomed off the coast of Newfoundland.

Meals consisted of dark, soggy potatoes,
meat they didn't recognize.

Men slept in hammocks in a large, open room.
Women and children had beds in small cabins.

In the evenings when the sea
was calm and the heavens clear,

Mama and Papa stood on deck,
shared stories with other immigrants

about who they wanted to become,
the lives and families they aimed to grow.

Their words became stars,
their dreams, a constellation guiding them

to a destination they hoped
would be worth the pain of leaving.

Immigrant Trails

The route Mama and Papa followed to America
was well worn by thousands of Swedish immigrants—

Gothenburg to Hull then Liverpool,
across the Atlantic to Quebec,

then Detroit, Chicago, Milwaukee,
and on to La Crosse, St. Paul and St. Cloud.

There they bought a wagon, a yoke of oxen,
two milk cows, a plow, and set out

on the Red River Trail,
an oxcart path cut by Indians.

Finally, they stopped in Ben Wade Township,
Pope County, Minnesota.

Thousands of miles of exodus and arrival
hewn into soil and sea by hardship and hope.

Thousands of stories of loss and expectancy
overheard by land and water.

Thousands of footsteps laying down
a path to a new destiny.

Alchemy of Possibility

After surviving the two-month journey to America
across the North Sea, through England,

across the Atlantic, up the St. Lawrence River,
through parts of Ontario and the Upper Midwest,

after traveling in three ships, six trains,
an oxen-pulled covered wagon,

after arriving at a new homestead's flat, marshy,
mostly treeless landscape, heartsick and weary,

after using her good arm to help Papa dig
a cave-like house into a hill and roof it with sod,

after breaking ground for a couple of acres of oats,
clearing a small plot for potatoes and a few vegetables,

after transforming a wagon box into a bed, a trunk
into a table, traveling bags and boxes into chairs,

Mama planted dahlias.
Before leaving Sweden, she'd wrapped the tubers

in old cloth, packed them in a trunk, hoping
they'd breathe air without getting drenched by the sea.

When she reached Minnesota, it was late June,
really too late to plant dahlias, but they were

her connection to Sweden.
Tiny packages preserving a familiar life.

When they bloomed, they'd be a sign that even
on a new continent, the alchemy

of earth, air, fire and water
could transform loss into possibility.

Finding Safe Harbor

Mama and Papa, her parents and her siblings
claimed six one-hundred-and-sixty-acre homesteads

through the Homestead Act of 1862.
Each was free except for a small filing fee

and the promise to "prove up" the land—
live on it, farm it, build a home on it.

The land was tallgrass prairie, rich, black soil
stretching the horizons in west central Minnesota.

It was land not totally unknown to them.
A friend from Sweden had settled

in Pope County the previous year.
A Swedish pastor they met in St. Paul

had assured them
it was a good place to farm.

Mama found the prairie frightening,
unnerving, like the ocean.

Standing on a knoll not far
from her sod house, turning around

to take in a place more sky
than earth, she felt herself

back onboard ship,
homesick, adrift, wondering,

How will I find myself
where there's no place to harbor?

Turning Fear into Mercy

Thousands of years of shadows wafted
through the tall grass—the shadows of

makers of tools,
gatherers of wild plants,

hunters of bison,
catchers of fish,

planters of corn, beans, squash and rice,
creators of clay vessels,

builders of burial mounds,
tellers of myths.

By the time Mama and her family claimed
their homesteads, most of the Dakota were gone.

The U.S. government had acquired their land
in an 1851 treaty that granted them

only a small sliver of land, leaving them starving
with no access to hunting grounds

and only a fraction of the promised payment.
After the Uprising of 1862, most were captured

executed, interned or banished.
Only a few remained.

Newcomers to the land
were warned to be afraid.

Mama's youngest brother, Henrik, described
the family's first evening on the open prairie:

> *That was a night never to be forgotten.*
> *It was frightfully cold and the grass*
>
> *was covered with frost.*
> *We had heard so much about*
>
> *the atrocities . . . and now we were*
> *in the midst of them, Indians on all sides.*
>
> *We didn't close our eyes in sleep that night.*
> *This was the wild west.*

Mama never lost her terror of the Dakota,
never overcame her alarm when they entered

her house unbidden, extended
their hands, begging for food.

When she could, she'd give them
what remained of the little she had.

After they left her house, she'd step
outside, look up at the blue sky,

pray the prairie sun was bright
enough to burn off the fear

that threatened her days,
leave only mercy behind.

A Threadbare History

A history of the first white settlers
in Pope County includes

the names of Grandpa Elias
and my papa, Andrew.*

It's a history of institutions founded,
buildings erected, men elected,

not the day-in, day-out, back-breaking
work of pioneering life.

In it there's no account of the grit
Mama had to summon to chase snakes

that slid down the mud walls of her dugout home,
keep its roof from collapsing when rain poured

through its holes, work in the fields and rest
at night while mosquitos gorged on her body.

There's no mention of the strength
it took Papa and Grandpa to prepare

for their first Minnesota winter—
haul logs fifteen miles in order to build a small,

ten- by fifteen-foot house and a makeshift barn,
hike forty miles to buy a pig and a few chickens,

use shovels to dig a well because
the slough water they drank would freeze.

It doesn't describe how Mama, her mother
and her sisters stored up food for the winter,

gathered potatoes, made bread from oats
they had planted, butchered and salted the pig,

dried wild herbs for tea, ground and roasted
bread crumbs and peas for makeshift coffee,

all the time knowing their meals would be meager—
a small portion of a potato with a tiny slice

of salt pork, savored at the table then put
into pockets to nibble on the rest of the day.

It's a threadbare history, too thin
to bear the weight of the immigrant spirit.

*By the 1875 census, Gedia's grandfather, Elias Bengtsson, had become Elias Benson, and her uncle, Henrik Bengtsson, Henry Benson. By the 1880 census, her father, Anders Petterson, had become Andrew Peterson.

Warming a Homesick Heart

Mama and her family survived their first winter
by sharing memories of Sweden—

Their last Yule with meatballs and sausages,
rice pudding and lingonberry relish served on

a table covered with newly spun white linens
and a straw harvest crown in the center;

homemade candles lighting every corner;
the scent of juniper and evergreen branches

strewn on floors scrubbed clean;
a freshly cut tree decorated with handcrafted ornaments;

the joy of linking hands with friends and neighbors
as everyone walked to church on Christmas morning.

The double wedding of Mama and her sister Klara,
the brides in mother-made gowns with long white veils

held in place with golden crowns;
the men in tailor-made suits and new shoes;

Papa's failed attempts at dancing with his new bride;
daily banquets at a week-long wedding feast.

Mama was desperate to hang on to
the laughter their words kindled.

She'd expected a brutal winter,
but not how strong the prairie wind could blow,

not how, without remorse, it whipped the cold
in and through everything in its path, lodging itself

stubbornly in her house and in her body.
She'd been ready for hard, bone-wearying work,

but not how poverty would scrape
her hands and her spirit raw.

As she reminisced with her family,
she stretched her cold arms around

their memories, pulled them into her chest, hoping
they'd kindle warmth in her homesick heart.

Saving Graces

In the spring Mama knelt down on land
she didn't know, dug in the ground

with hands she didn't recognize,
and replanted her Swedish dahlias

that had bloomed the past summer,
survived the bitter winter.

Covering them with dirt, she prayed
she would take on their resilience,

find the courage to set down firm roots
in strange surroundings, gather strength

from the earth and blossom.
Mama missed the flowers of her Swedish countryside—

the delicate forget-me-nots reminding her
to cherish moments thought too brief to matter,

the lilies-of-the-valley whose sweet tiny bells
tolled the grace of small things,

the white preacher's collar daisies whose yellow
centers assured her the sun would always return.

Just when she felt her homesickness
would never thaw, the world turned

and pale blue crocuses popped up
everywhere in the dry prairie grass.

Wild.
Unexpected.

Could they somehow have known
they saved her?

Wait Upon the Lord

The arrival of more settlers,
many of them friends and relatives

from Mama's home province in Sweden,
eased her homesickness,

but Papa and Grandpa knew
there was only one thing they could do

to warm the soul winter had chilled—
build Mama a church, the Norunga church,

a small log structure with a plain pulpit and altar
named after their parish church in Sweden.

When it was finished, men and women sat on hand-made
benches on opposite sides of the sanctuary—

men in overalls, white linen shirts with stiff paper collars,
black cravats and cowboy boots,

women in homespun skirts covered with aprons,
psalm books wrapped inside handkerchiefs tucked

into their pockets, their heads hidden
under checkered cotton scarfs.

As the pastor delivered his sermon in Swedish,
men chewed tobacco, lowered

their faces to sniff a pinch of snuff
taken from their vest pockets.

Across the aisle, women bowed
their heads in prayer.

Papa always said he owed
his faith to Mama.

> It was because of her I became
> conscious of my sins.

> She was so much better than I was,
> so sincere in her convictions.

In Sweden, Mama had gone to revival meetings
in private homes for prayer and study.

After one such gathering, one Papa attended
with "a bunch of rowdies" who wanted

to disrupt and not to worship,
Mama confronted him,

> The Lord was in our midst.
> How could you act so?

Papa saw it as the turning point in his life.
From then on he made sure to pay attention

as Mama read the Bible to their children, join in
when she recited her favorite verse:

> *But they that wait upon the Lord shall renew*
> *their strength; they shall mount up with wings*
>
> *as eagles; they shall run, and not be weary;*
> *and they shall walk, and not faint.*

Waiting upon the Lord.
It became the lodestar for Papa's life.

Sitting in the new church, looking across
the aisle at Mama, light coming in

through the plain glass windows
streaming down on the top of her head,

he knew, given time, she would remember
it was hers as well.

Finding Solace for a Lost Soul

My grandma Johanna, Mama's step-mother,
had a kind and gentle way about her,

the perfect personality for a healer
who delivered babies,

soothed headaches, treated toothaches,
and patched up torn muscles.

Practical and down-to-earth,
she was a practitioner of cupping

who made cuts on her patient's arm or shoulder,
then applied a heated glass cup

to suction blood and relieve congestion.
And when she felt the situation called for it,

she was a no-nonsense bloodletter who carried
three-inch long, dark maroon leeches in water bottles

at the bottom of her medicine bag
to lay on skin and suck out infection.

If only she could have found something in her satchel
to draw the darkness from Mama's spirit,

alleviate what Mama called her "attacks"—
debilitating bouts of depression

that siphoned the life out of her.
Grandma prescribed tonics with names

like "St. Jacob's Oil," "Wizard Oil," "Stomach Bitters"
and a strange concoction called "Beef, Iron and Wine."

Sometimes they helped, but more often than not,
only time's passing permitted Mama

to take up her life again.
Then seeing Mama return to her self,

Grandma would get down on her knees,
thank God for her daughter's recovery,

pray that when the next "attack" came,
she'd have just the right elixir

to prevent Mama from slipping away again.
And if for some reason God didn't show her

the cure, she'd lower herself to her knees,
plead with God to guard the woman she loved,

hold her in safekeeping until once again,
her cherished daughter could find her way home.

Looking for the Promised Land

I have always envied my oldest siblings—
Johan Emil, Selma Elizabeth and Ida Charlotte—

for carrying Swedish soil in their bones,
the scent of her green forests in their lungs.

The thought of their connection
to our homeland never failed

to set me dreaming of a place
I would never see.

These three siblings were joined in close
succession by three children born

in the first five years on the Minnesota prairie—
Carl Oscar, Leonard (who died in infancy)

and Minnie Christine who was born a few days
after the historic Easter Blizzard of 1873.

An epic storm barreling out of the Dakota prairies,
it overtook Papa, his brother, and Mama's uncle

on one of their fifteen-mile treks to get wood.
All survived, but only barely.

Mama, nine months pregnant, alone
at the homestead with the children,

came close to losing her way in the snow
when, to keep her young ones warm,

she ventured outside, tore down a shed
and sawed its boards to burn for heat.

Hot weather brought its own destruction
when later that summer, swarms of grasshoppers

swooped in to cover the prairie, eating vegetation
and destroying crops, invading homes,

chewing off handles on tools left outside.
Papa set out large pans of tar to catch the locusts,

pleaded with God when his efforts failed.
At wits' end, he asked himself,

> Can it be right to raise a family
> in such surroundings?

Convinced it wasn't, he bought a lot in Alexandria,
a fast-growing community some twenty-five miles away,

built a two-room frame house
and moved his family there in 1876.

They had risked everything to come to America,
hung their future on a tiny sliver of possibility,

darned if now, he was going to give up,
give in to thinking it impossible.

That wasn't his way.
He wasn't Moses,

but he was determined to deliver his family
out of the prairie's hard hands.

And if they didn't find the promised land?
At least they'd settle in a place

where there was enough promise
to keep their hope alive.

Finding Welcome

When Mama, a woman with farming
in her bones, was a few years shy of forty,

she found herself moving to a town,
a freshly minted town, a collection of stores

and log cabins, small homes and tar paper shacks
edged by lakes and bordered on the east by woods.

There she found a busy world—
a world banded by narrow boardwalks running

in front of a general store, a court house, a city hotel,
a bank, a blacksmith shop, a flour mill, a meat market,

a gun shop, a couple of churches and a few saloons;
a world divided into a smörgåsbord of cultures—

Swedish, German, Norwegian, Finnish and Danish,
Bohemian, Irish and Yankees from eastern states;

a world clannish and segregated, yet connected
by hard work and hope.

She also found women, women to talk to,
gossip with, ask for advice;

women who came together to make bread,
piece quilts, trade clothing patterns;

women to grow old with,
keep her from feeling alone;

women who welcomed her to a place
they were trying their best to call home.

Shouldering the Weight

Mama drew strength from her new surroundings,
felt herself heal as she breathed in the beauty

of green leaves and bird song, gain energy
as she soaked up the swirl and bustle of living in town.

Needing to create an income for his family,
Papa sold the small house he had built,

bought another one, then enlarged it
so they could take in boarders—

men working on the railroads,
farmers hauling grain to town elevators,

laborers serving on threshing crews—
each one paying twelve dollars a month

to live at the Peterson Boarding House,
sleep on straw ticks on bunk beds in a converted barn,

eat simple suppers of soup and bread, custard and
coffee, take filled lunch pails to work every morning.

It didn't take long before there were twenty-five residents,
too many for Mama to tend on her own,

so she turned to her two oldest daughters,
Selma Elizabeth and Ida Charlotte,

young teenagers at the time, to help her plan
and prepare meals, shop for food and wash dishes,

boil the men's clothes to rid them of lice,
dust the house and polish furniture,

sweep floors, sew and mend,
clean and fill twenty-five lunch pails.

And when she gave birth to Clarence Edward
in 1875, and three years later, her final child,

Hulda Egedia (Gedia), the author of this story,
Mama relied on her two youngest children,

Carl Oscar and Minnie Christine to rock their cradles,
and her oldest son, John Emil, to run errands,

fill kerosene lamps, clean chimneys and polish kettles.
Everyone was expected to pitch in, share the weight,

their duty to family, a gift of love
they gave their mother.

A Future Bigger Than Hope Can See

Free as the Prairie Wind

Mama was forty-one when I was born on May 2, 1878.
If she'd hoped her last child would be quiet

and reserved, a daughter cast in her own mold,
she must've been surprised, for I was strong-willed,

stubborn and fiercely independent, a "dust devil"
skedaddling across the prairie on a plank

drawn by a horse whose reins were held by a young man
thirteen years my senior, a farm laborer,

a resident at the Peterson Boarding House,
Gustaf Elof Johnson, the man I would one day marry.

Flying over the ground, holding the board's edges
so tightly my knuckles turned white

(as white as Mama's face
if she'd seen me),

I'd scream at the top of my lungs,
yell at Elof to make the horse go faster.

> *Give me the reins.*
> *I can do it myself.*

But he always refused.
Nothing was going to happen

to Mama's youngest daughter, no matter
how much I pestered and pouted.

I was nine when twenty-two-year-old Elof
arrived in Alexandria, my free

and fun-loving spirit a good match
for his dreamy idealism, his fascination

with words and ideas, a reservoir
for the learning I'd grow into wanting.

But reading and writing were for another time.
At nine, all I wanted to do was ride

like the wind, sail on my plank till it lifted
off the ground and set me free.

A Love Never Finished

When I was fourteen, my parents gave me
the choice of attending high school

or quitting to help Mama tend to boarders
and take care of the house.

I chose to stay home, spend
what little spare time I had

riding horses (now that I was old enough
to handle them) and reading poetry,

a rather surprising desire
I'd acquired from Elof.

Later in life, I couldn't remember a time
when I didn't love poetry,

a time when I didn't love Elof.
My favorite poem, Bourdillon's "Light," begins,

>	*The night has a thousand eyes*

and ends,

>	*Yet the light of a whole life dies*
>	*When its love is done.*

In the margins of my copy I wrote,

> *Elof, it will never*
> *be done.*

Now I know, for certain,
it never will.

A Believer

The man I loved was a land-poor man,
a farm laborer born on November 1, 1865,

a young man in his early twenties when he followed
his uncles and their families to Alexandria in 1887.

He was a visionary man looking to America
for land and livelihood;

a religious man, a believer in the Second Coming,
who wanted freedom to practice his Baptist faith;

a hopeful man who trusted he would land
in America with God and good fortune on his side;

a confident man who believed he could wrench
possibility out of an improbable story.

The Counsel of Friends

Soon after my Elof arrived in Alexandria, he joined
the Swedish Baptist Church, the same congregation

where his cousins and my family belonged.
Some years before, Mama and Papa had left

the Lutheran Church for the Baptist Church,
an abandonment condemned by their former pastor:

> *Andrew Peterson and wife have fallen*
> *into a deep confusion.*
>
> *He is nothing more*
> *than a rotted carcass.*

But they weren't confused, and neither was Elof.
What they found on the other side

of their church's tall, white doors was a young
spiritual community that listened to services

in Swedish, studied scriptures every Sabbath,
and carried on lively discussions about salvation.

For Elof, newcomer to America, it was a place to find
friends who, during his first decade in America,

filled his small, red-velvet autograph book
with verse and prose, in English and Swedish,

wishing him a good and God-filled life.
My brother Edward wrote:

> *The world stretches brightly before you*
> *A field for your muscle and brain*
>
> *And though clouds may often float over you*
> *And often comes tempest and rain*
>
> *Be fearless of storms which o're take you*
> *Push forward through all like a man*
>
> *Good fortune will never forsake you*
> *If you do as near right as you can.*

Another friend advised:

> *I cannot wish thee greater joys,*
> *Than others here expressed,*
>
> *But I respond with every power,*
> *To wish thee ever blessed.*

Offering more counsel,
someone penned:

Let the road be rough and dreary,
And its end far out of sight;

Foot it bravely—strong or weary—
Trust in God, and do the right.

Elof kept his autograph book beside
his bed next to his Bible—

the words of his friends,
a call to walk the path of righteousness,

the Word of God,
a beacon that would light his way.

Music's Solace

Elof had been in America almost
a decade when, in the summer of 1894,

he received a black-banded letter
from his sister Augusta:

> *Papa has gone home and away from us.*
> *We feel it is so empty and sad with him gone.*
>
> *But we know at the same time,*
> *we are grateful that*
>
> *he is with our dear Father*
> *and that his soul is saved forever.*

Believing that some day he and his Papa
would meet again comforted Elof,

but in his grief, he knew of only one way
to keep his Papa close—

pick up his violin, pull the bow
across the strings, lay bare

the sorrow he couldn't find
words to speak.

To this day, I can hear his music, see him sway
as he stood in the parlor and played.

Melodies—hymns he knew,
tunes he had heard,

phrases born in his imagination—
poured out of him as if the One

who spins music out of stars,
breath out of spirit,

was moving his fingers,
flying his bow.

Later, when I asked him
about the river his heartache

had set free, he said
he couldn't remember

where he had gone
or the current he had sailed.

He only knew
he hadn't been there alone.

Words of Kindness and Kinship

It wasn't only sadness over
his Papa's death that Elof read

in his sister's letter.
Augusta missed her brother:

> *Won't you come home to us in the fall*
> *while we feel so alone?*
>
> *You can go back to America in the spring*
> *if you want to.*

There was pain in her words, pain Elof
had caused by not writing more often:

> *Papa waited for a letter from you*
> *many times. He managed to talk*
>
> *about wanting a letter from you*
> *even though in the end, he was very weak.*

Elof vowed to be a better brother
than he was a son.

He'd write to his sister.
Send her his words.

Openhearted, generous,
kind-spirited words,

words that would bear a brother's love
no matter how great the distance between them.

Words like rays from far-off sun
shimmering on a wind-ruffled lake,

reminding water
sun is kin.

A Future Hope Can't See

In 1895 Elof delivered the class prophecy
at the graduation ceremony marking

his matriculation from night classes
in English and the three R's

held for adults at the Lake Geneva school
(District 22 school in Alexandria Township).

Taking his place in front of his classmates,
many of them immigrants like himself, Elof began:

> *Well, here before you I stand tonight.*
> *I may tell you, I have been trembling.*
>
> *My heart has not been delight.*
> *I was doomed to solve a question,*
>
> *One of the hardest and most difficult*
> *Ever put before me in my life.*
>
> *It was concerning the lifting of the veil*
> *That hides the future for the class of ninety-five.*
>
> *Who can gaze into the future?*
> *Who can tell of days we have not seen?*

I'm only a man of mortal nature,
The path of my thoughts is not always serene.

Yet did I think so much of this question,
So much, still I do to you declare

That I came to no decision,
I was about to give it up in despair.

Written on small sheets of lined paper,
his penmanship clean and curvaceous,

his surefooted English peppered with Latin,
German and Italian phrases, the speech describes

how Elof, inspired by a vision and the voice of God,
makes an imaginary trip to Germany where he meets

the future selves of two of his classmates.
The first, the captain of his steamer:

A captain like him was not to be seen. . . .
He was the bravest captain that has ever been.

The second, a famous musician
on the stage in Hamburg:

He sang and played about our love . . .
It swelled as though coming from above.

It's not until Elof pictures himself safely back
in Minnesota that he discovers his own future:

> *There I tell you I saw someone like a real fool.*
> *It was St. Paul's noted rag peddler*
>
> *Who drove around with his little cart and mule.*
> *What foolish rag peddler,*
>
> *Thought on his way to fame.*
> *But someone told me, if he should not get it,*
>
> *He only had his nose to blame. Who was he?*
> *you seem to wonder. And wish that man to see.*
>
> *Of course you can, don't wait any longer,*
> *You will see him now, if you look at me.*

Listening to Elof deliver his speech,
I wondered why he saw himself this way.

Was he too humble to predict his own success?
Too fearful he might anger fate?

Too worried, that at thirty,
his future might be behind him?

Perhaps it was that the future he'd crossed
the ocean to find wasn't possible . . . yet.

Perhaps it was going to take a new century
with new land opened up for homesteading,

with new machinery to farm it
to give Elof that possibility.

Perhaps in the twentieth century, he'd find
a future his nineteenth-century hope couldn't see.

A Pledge of Forever

I was seventeen in 1895 (the same year
as Elof's class prophecy)

when I wrote this prayer
in his tiny, red-velvet autograph book:

> *Smoothly down life's ebbing tide,*
> *May our vessels safely glide,*
>
> *And may we anchor*
> *side-by-side in Heaven.*

I signed it,

> *Your friend.*

Three years later, Elof matched
my words in one of many

love poems he finally
felt free to share with me:

Dearest, dearest sweetheart, my heart is full
Of dearest love, God give us heavenly tides,

That our little vessel smoothly lull,
With you, forever, at my side.

He addressed it,

    My beloved.

Together. Forever.
Smooth and safe.

It was our prayer.
It would be our salvation.

A Waiting Man

Elof was a waiting man.
He'd waited to emigrate from Sweden

until he was old enough to join
his cousins in America,

waited to declare his love for me
until I turned twenty,

waited to marry me until land
opened up he could buy.

Land had always been a magnet for Elof.
First there had been land in the tallgrass prairie

of Minnesota, land he couldn't afford to buy
when he got there in 1887.

Then, as one century ended
and a new one began,

land opened up in Canada,
land for homesteading

on her Western plains, land
for land-poor folks like us.

Canada wanted us.
The railroads wanted us to settle prairies, grow

the economy, expand the country westward.
Advertising was everywhere—

in newspapers, on postcards and posters,
printed in pamphlets at farm shows.

There's good land, they said. *No greater grain-growing
land than in Canada's Prairie Provinces.*

The last best West, they called it.
Come help turn grassland into the world's granary.

Conditions couldn't be better, they promised.
The depression has ended. Wheat prices are rising.

You'll have everything you need, they pledged.
Miles of rails to transport you and your wheat.

*New machinery. New ways to farm that don't require
much water. Hardier wheat seeds.*

It's just what my land-poor Elof had waited for—
a door to our future, the means to swing it open,

and the opportunity to transform his dream
into a story we both could write.

It was time for us to marry, go to Canada,
take advertising at its word.

Head First into the Future

A simple invitation on a plain ivory card.
A simple home ceremony.

> *Mr. and Mrs. A. P. Peterson*
> *request your presence*
>
> *at the marriage of their daughter,*
> *Hulda Egedia to Gustave E. Johnson,*
>
> *Thursday, April twenty-third,*
> *nineteen hundred and three, at seven o'clock p.m.*
>
> *Alexandria, Minnesota.*
> *Corner F Street and Third Avenue.*

I was almost twenty-five.
Elof was thirty-seven.

Our wedding picture shows no age difference,
no hint of hesitancy between us, no hidden secrets

or selves kept out of sight, only an ease
born of a friendship eighteen years in the making.

Elof & Gedia, wedding (1903, Alexandria, MN)

Elof stares straight into the camera, eyebrows raised,
a quixotic gleam in his dark eyes, an exuberance

simmering below the surface.
Handsome in his tails, watch tucked into his vest,

white bow tie circling his high shirt collar,
he's eager to exit the frame, start our new life together.

I'm in a frothy, frilly, puff-of-a-dress
with yards of muslin billowing to the floor,

gathering in flouncy layers around the hem of my skirt.
Ruffles encircle the high neck of my blousy bodice,

gird the cuffs of my ballooning sleeves.
A crown of flowers anchors a long, gauzy veil

garnished with myrtle from Mama's porch garden—
sprigs of good fortune for love everlasting.

I dangle a small bouquet in my left hand,
slip my right through Elof's arm, not grasping,

just resting, trusting, relaxed.
My gaze, strong and self-assured, looks past

the camera, my energy, like Elof's,
impatient to move into the future.

There is no fear in my face nor in Elof's,
no slackness in our posture,

only a certainty that having safely sailed
love's tides for so long, we would let

no storm unmoor us
from each other's side.

Strong Enough to Bend Without Breaking

In another wedding photo,
Elof looks off into the distance.

His face is clean shaven
except for a wisp of a mustache;

his dark hair, side-parted
and slicked back, forms a slight

Elof, wedding portrait

pompadour above his forehead.
It is a graceful, finely chiseled face,

handsome and elegant; a face of a poet or a philosopher
unweathered by the hard work of farming;

a face of a gentle man whose eyes carry nothing
but optimism, whose jaw allows nothing but confidence;

a face sculpted by faith, showing no memory
of battles fought, no fear of shadows to come.

Unassailable.
Strong.

The face of a man supple enough to suffer
an unknown future without breaking.

Finding Our Place

Elof filed a claim for land
in Canada's Western plains —

one quarter section of land
a half-mile square,

one hundred and sixty acres
in the District of Assiniboia,

five hundred miles northwest of Alexandria,
fifty miles north of the Canada-North Dakota border.

In return for our square of earth,
we paid a small registration fee

and promised the government
we'd "prove it up" —

cultivate the land, build a permanent
dwelling on it within three years.

> *Of course we'll live there,*
> I said to Elof.

> *Where else does the government think*
> *we're gonna live?*

Elof always had such patience,
especially with me. He had to.

A farmer can't survive without patience.
Neither can a husband.

When I stop to think about it,
Elof was a mixture of patience

and a let's-get-it-done-now attitude.
It just depended on what he was up against,

and that spring, he was keen to leave Alexandria,
catch prime plowing and planting time in Canada.

So he bought two tickets for a train leaving on May 4,
only a week and a half after our wedding,

two days after my twenty-fifth birthday.
For our fare, a fare made cheap by the railroad

so homesteaders could afford to take all their belongings,
we had half a railroad car for our four head of cattle,

four horses and stock feed; half a car
for our wagon, farm equipment, fence supplies,

seed grain, household goods and food stuff;
and two seats in the "colonist" car,

a car with pull-down sleeping berths
and a kitchen I could use.

> *It'll more than do,*
> I told Elof.

It was a long, stuffy, bumpy trip, every seat taken
by people from more countries than we could name,

air filled to bursting with the aroma of strange food
and languages we didn't understand.

When finally the train pulled into a baby-of-a-town,
a town we'd soon name Midale,

we unloaded our property, tied up our animals
and tried to sleep in an empty railroad car

left alongside the tracks by officials.
I don't think either one of us slept.

Too excited. Too tired.
Too much unknown.

In the morning, we set out to find our land,
using a compass to calculate direction,

counting the revolutions of a rag tied
to a wagon wheel to gauge distance.

It was well past noon before we spotted
the survey mound and stake marking the location

of our homestead—North East section 32,
township 05, range 10 west of the second Meridian.

Overcome with gratitude for land
that was ours, Elof and I knelt down,

planted our palms on the warm,
spring ground, promised God we'd seed

love as well as wheat in the soil
He'd entrusted to us.

> *Forever, Gedia,*
> Elof said as he helped me up.

Standing with him, I looked over our land,
filled my lungs with sun and blue sky.

For a moment, the emptiness disoriented me.
But far from the dread that had overcome

Mama when she first saw Minnesota's
unbounded prairie, I relished

the grassland's openness, its freedom,
its unharnessed energy.

I knew I could grow a family there,
on that earth, under that sun.

    I am made for this place,
    I thought.

Turning to my new husband,
I smiled.

    Yes, Elof,
    forever.

When Uncertainty Becomes Possibility

The work of setting up a homestead
and helping build a new town

would not be ours alone.
Many from Alexandria had joined us—

my youngest brother, Edward,
and his soon-to-be-wife, Annie Charlotta,

several of Elof's cousins and their families,
almost the entire membership of our First Baptist Church.

Years later, a friend sent me a history of the town
written for its semi-centennial:

> *In the early summer of 1903, a number of settlers*
> *arrived in what later became known as Midale . . .*

> *These settlers looked at the vast open prairie*
> *with optimism and courage.*

Optimism.
Courage.

Exactly what we needed to give birth
to a new settlement where none had existed.

Exactly what it would take to keep going
when we found the land harder to farm

than we imagined, the climate more brutal
than we anticipated, the price of grain

more unpredictable
than we expected.

Exactly what was essential
to call forth in each other,

trusting that if we tempered our optimism
with common sense, our courage with caution,

God would help us stretch
uncertainty into possibility.

Bees

Rolling up our sleeves,
joining with our family and friends,

we set out to work.
Houses were raised,

barns were built,
grassland was broken, together.

Rocks were moved, trees were felled,
soil was plowed, together.

Wheat was sowed, cut and combined,
stoked and threshed, together.

We called them "bees" —
a barn-raising bee, a sodding bee,

a bee to break the land,
a bee to do just about everything.

"Bees." A funny word
that for us meant "prayer."

So every time we had a bee,
we started by bowing

our heads, acknowledging
that our work was both

an answer to a prayer
and the prayer itself.

Prairie Determination

In those days, I was as strong
as a horse, stocky

and powerful with energy
that never wilted.

I loved to work outside—
drive the oxen team, turn the soil over,

sow a field, feed the chickens,
plant a vegetable garden, milk the cows,

dig a well, wash clothes over a fire,
hang them on a line to dry.

The more I worked under
the prairie sun, absorbed

the open fields, the more I filled
my chest with the freedom

I'd sought as a young girl
flying down a dirt path

on a horse-drawn plank
with Elof holding the reins.

I was a no-nonsense, no-grumbling,
no-time-like-the-present kind of woman.

Determined.
Stubborn.

A woman who learned
during her first summer in Canada

that she would wield any shovel,
lift any hammer, move any earth

to make a home for Elof
and the child she was carrying.

Singing Our Way to the Promised Land

With all there was still to do before winter set in,
we took a break from field-tending and house-raising

to found the First Swedish Baptist Church of Midale,
the oldest church in Saskatchewan.

Elof and I, along with my brother Edward,
were charter members.

Our preacher, Reverend Olaf Sutherland,
had come with us from Alexandria.

"Singing Ole," we called him.
To this day I can hear him leading us,

feel how we shook the sanctuary
with our joyful noise—

on-key, off-key, some of us in-between-keys,
all of us bellowing with every ounce of breath we had.

But it wasn't just *our* breath.
Somehow "Singing Ole" invited

the breath of our Creator to join us,
and it was our music,

as out-of-tune as it was,
that brought our tired bones to life.

Prairie Resolve

When the weather turned cold, I thought
about Mama's first winter in Minnesota,

how she prepared for it by planting
potatoes, making bread, salting a pig,

how Papa and his brothers cleared ground for oats,
hauled lumber to build a cabin, dug a well for fresh water,

how they came close to starving,
how the dark days drowned Mama in depression.

But I was stronger than Mama, gut-sure I would get us
through the winter no matter how hard it was.

And it was harder than I'd imagined,
hard enough to humble even me.

We did all we could—
covered our floors and walls with rugs,

stuffed rags into cracks around doors,
hung curtains on windows.

But it wasn't enough.
Mornings we woke to hoarfrost so thick

on the inside of windows and walls,
the underside of the bed,

we had to scrape it off into pails.
Blizzards piled snow to the roof.

Wind deposited snow inside, pushing it
through openings we thought we'd sealed.

Outside, animals needed tending,
water needed fetching,

paths needed shoveling,
the outhouse needed visiting.

But I wasn't discouraged.
The cold stiffened my will, froze

my backbone as straight as the sheets
slapping on the clothesline outside our door.

> *We will make it through this,* I said to Elof
> as we huddled under every blanket we owned.

Rolling over, he stroked
my swollen belly.

> *I pray our child has your resolve, Gedia.*
> *No one survives on this prairie without it.*

Reunion

A little lamb sits atop his tombstone
guarding these words:

> *Carl Emanuel*
> *Infant Son of Gustave E. and Egedia Johnson*
>
> *Born March 30, 1904*
> *Died April 20, 1904*
>
> *Budded on earth*
> *to bloom in Heaven.*

The lamb's face looks out over the tiny grave
straight into the eyes of the visitor,

a symbol of both the innocent child
and the Shepherd who would hoist

the young sheep on his shoulders
and carry him home.

We named our son "Carl" to honor
one of my older brothers,

"Emanuel" so he would grow up knowing
God was with him.

Now it would remind us
he was with God.

We fought our way through our grief
by singing it out loud:

> What tho' griefs and care encumber,
> Weary burdens press me long,

> When His kindness I remember,
> This shall ever be my song.

> In the Everlasting Arms,
> In the Everlasting Arms,

> We shall find eternal refuge
> In the Everlasting Arms.

As our voices wrung out the sadness
in our souls, as we wailed our despair

in words we had the strength
to sing, but not to say,

we found refuge for ourselves,
reunion with our son.

The Way of the World

Our grief was heavy.
It wrapped its arms

around our necks, distorted
how we sat and slept,

how we ate
and did our chores.

It blocked our view
of the sun and each other.

We read favorite Bible verses, prayed
till we had no words left,

sang hymns with our friends
till our throats were dry.

But still our grief hung on.

At night, we stood in silence
under the stars, hoped

that listening to the sounds of life
on the prairie might help.

But still our grief hung on.

Elof picked up his violin.
Maybe his music would take

some of our sorrow with it
as it disappeared over the horizon.

But still our grief hung on.

> *It's the way of the world,*
> I said to Elof.

He looked at me, grief's shadow
shading his eyes.

> *I'm not surrendering, Elof,*
> *I'm accepting,*
>
> *accepting that in this world the weight*
> *of loss will always be here,*
>
> *accepting that sometimes it'll grow*
> *heavy, sometimes grow light,*
>
> *accepting I'm not immune to hardship,*
> *that no one, least of all God, is to blame.*

I had lost my first son.
Accepting his death

as the way of this world, knowing
it would be different in the next,

I felt grief start
to loosen her grip.

God's Doing

After the spring melt passed,
and the prairie was once again

more soil than soup,
we had much to do—

acres to clear and sod to break,
seeds to sow and firebreaks to plow,

fences to build and roofs to repair,
oxen to feed and cows to milk,

chickens to tend and hogs to slop,
vegetables to plant and weeds to hoe.

As slow, sweet rain moistened
our seedlings, as blue skies

encouraged them to break ground,
raise their tender green heads

into the light, we felt ourselves linked
with ancient alchemists turning

seed and sun, rain and earth
into grain as valuable as gold.

Perhaps it was because he was tired
of carrying sorrow's heavy load.

Perhaps his grief and fatigue
played with his thinking,

whatever the reason,
Elof became enchanted

with the young wheat shoots
pushing through the soil.

He could've stood over them
till the Lord came again if I'd let him.

    Elof, what are you doing?
    I asked him.

He struggled to pull
himself away.

    I'm wondering if it's love.

    If what's love? I said.

    If these small green babies are being
    called to life because of love.

I think it's God's doing, Elof.

Of course it's God's doing, Gedia.
But what if the way of God's doing is love?

I think he decided it was,
for slowly, as the summer wore on,

as his young green charges
grew into tall, sturdy wheat,

the sadness that had surrounded him
since the death of our son began to lift.

Standing Over the World in Amazement

Elof was a keen weather watcher,
a predictor of storms,

a reader of wind and clouds,
a diviner of rain and drought.

A few days after our son's death,
he started a daily journal—

a couple of lines about the weather
and our crops, brief comments

about the day's events and news
he had heard, written in Swedish

in a hurried script on the lined pages
of a tiny black book.

It became his crystal ball, a source
for information about what soil feels like

when it's time to plant, how air
gives warning a heavy frost

is just around the corner, what wind
smells like when a storm is picking up.

When Elof began his journal,
he said it helped him know

his place in the world, how small
he was, how insignificant.

But as the days of watching
and writing grew into weeks,

as the weeks of trying to figure out
what the earth was telling him

turned into years, Elof came to know
how big his place really was.

> *Gedia, when I study the color*
> *of the sky or the texture*
>
> *of the air on my skin,*
> *when I listen for changes*
>
> *in bird song or read how clouds*
> *are being sculpted,*
>
> *I am the world*
> *seeing herself.*

Of course you are, Elof.
The world longs for our attention.

Exactly, he nodded.
And how shall we respond to the world?

With amazement,
dear one.

Being Human

During the evenings, when Elof wrote
in his journal or played his violin,

I picked up my crocheting work.
No matter how tired I was, I couldn't end my day

without my hooks and my thread—
tonics for my tired bones and a troubled mind.

Doilies and shawls, tablecloths and runners,
edgings for handkerchiefs, trim for pillowcases,

piece after piece emerged from my hands,
each one, detailed and delicate, each one,

a universe of circles, swirls and spirals.
As I caught each loop with my hook, watched

thread-thin galaxies take shape in my lap,
I sensed myself being pulled into the patterns

I was crocheting, felt the comfort of being enveloped
in a web of creation, knew I was feeling

the same awe Elof experienced
when he wrote his daily observations.

Putting my work down, I glanced
at Elof, noticed the lines

that in the last months, sorrow
had etched on his wind-roughened face.

> *Grief's handiwork,*
> I said to him.

> Surprised, he looked up.
> *What is, my dear?*

> *Your face. Grief's had her hand*
> *on it. Mine, too, I reckon.*

> *Of course she has, Gedia.*

Then he asked his favorite question,

> *And how shall we respond to the world?*

I picked up our Bible with one hand,
put my other hand on Elof's heart.

> *The only way we can, dear one.*

Where God Lives

Sometimes Elof watched as I crocheted, intrigued
that I was able to connect separate shapes

into one design serving one particular function—
covering a table, decorating a dresser,

or catching dust, as he used to tease.
One evening he seemed particularly interested.

> *Gedia, our lives are like*
> *that doily,* he said.

> *My goodness, Elof, I hope you're not thinking*
> *we're only good to catch dust.*

He smiled.

> *No, what I mean is . . .*
> *Take a look at the spirals and how*

> *you've stitched them together.*
> *You've made a community, and so have we.*

And what a community we were!
There was our good friend Reverend Olaf Sutherland.

Lord have mercy, he could tell a good sermon,
raise us out of our seats with his voice,

drop us to our knees with his words.
And he had a right good head for business,

partnering with two other church members,
Olaf Wedin and Andrew Westman,

to form the Midale Mercantile Company.
Without them, we wouldn't have had

our general store, post office,
lumber yard or grain elevator.

Then there was John Anderson,
founder of Midale's first blacksmith shop,

a jack-of-all-trades who could do
just about anything he set his mind to.

He'd operated a sawmill in Alexandria with
the Reverend and had hauled a heap of lumber

to Canada so we could build our houses.
Every time Elof and I walked into our home,

we thanked John we had a door
and a house to go with it.

We wouldn't have had much of a school
if it hadn't been for Sven Jern, who served

as its caretaker, and Albin Erickson, Elof's cousin,
who was a member of the school board.

And there wouldn't have been a Baptist church
if it hadn't been for us.

Edward, my brother, was treasurer.
Elof was clerk.

As for the women in our group—
women like Carrie Sutherland and Albertina Wedin,

Ida Westman, Greta Anderson and Annie Jern,
Gerda Erickson and Annie Peterson—

all I can say is prairie living wouldn't be worth
a hill of beans without prairie women.

Elof looked up from the doily
he'd been studying.

> *It's beautiful, Gedia,*
> *especially the connections.*

> *You're right,* I said.
> *That's where God lives.*

Keeping Watch

Among Elof's things when he died
was a scrap of faded paper four decades old

tucked inside his autograph book. On it,
a penciled note in a child's uncertain script:

> *My Dear Papa,*
> *Your loving dear Florence sends*
>
> *so many hugs and kisses*
> *to my dear Papa, little Florence*

Florence Hildegard, born September 30, 1905,
was her father's daughter.

A musician.
A dreamer.

Tenacious when she took hold of something she loved,
especially when it was making music with her Papa.

Why, she'd have practiced our piano
from sunup till sundown if we'd let her.

My brother Edward loved to tell the story about how,
after we got telephone service in 1911,

Florence and Elof would call him and his wife, Annie,
not to talk, but to show-off the hymns they'd rehearsed.

Elof said it was because he wanted to make sure
the new-fangled phone lines carried music.

I think it was because
he was proud of his daughter.

Florence had two brothers—
Reubin Ellsworth, born February 28, 1908,

and Gordon Eugene, born December 10, 1910.
They were as smart as all get out.

Reubin, an affectionate little tyke,
thoughtful and quiet like his Papa;

Gordon, so good at figuring things out,
an engineer, even as a child.

Edward's and Annie's family was growing as well—
Gladys Adeline, Clarence, Della Ruth,

Waldo, and Desmer Wallace.
Sometimes I'd look at our children playing

together, imagine Carl Emmanuel in their midst.
Then I'd remember the little lamb on his tombstone,

close my eyes and pray the good Shepherd
was keeping a close watch over all our little ones.

Striking Water from a Rock

Elof wouldn't take no for an answer.
Our wheat was growing,

the weather was cooperating, and life
was calling him to celebrate.

> *Gedia, you and Annie can help*
> *get the food together.*

> *Edward and I will set up the tables.*
> *I'll take my violin.*

> *We'll sing hymns.*
> *Maybe we'll even have a baseball game.*

So one day in midsummer, dressed
in our Sunday best, our wagons and buggies full,

Elof and I and our friends set out to have a picnic.
It was a fine day, warm, not too hot,

the bluest of blue sky with a breeze
taking its time to sashay across the prairie.

We had enough food for the whole province—
cold baked ham and fried chicken,

potato salad and coleslaw,
jellied fruit and pickled beets,

breads and buns and rolls,
cakes, pies and cookies.

Every bit of it the best
anyone had ever tasted,

or so said every man there.
Of course, there wasn't a woman among us

who hadn't saved her finest meats,
her freshest vegetables for the picnic.

As we ate, our talk meandered from weather
and crops to children and their schooling.

The more we talked, the more we realized
that no matter how parched from heartache

we might be, no matter how dry
the future might sometimes look,

our friendship tapped a deep spring,
quenching the isolation of prairie living.

The picnic became a bookmark
in my memory, a place

I turned to every time I needed
reminding it's love

that strikes water from
a rock in the desert.

Tears in Her Eyes

Edward and I were the only
Peterson children to move to Canada.

My other five siblings stayed close
to our Minnesota home, guaranteeing

Mama and Papa a good number
of grandchildren to keep them company.

When all of us gathered together
(Edward's family and mine went back

to Minnesota as often as we could),
we were quite a large and boisterous clan—

more than forty adults and children.
Everyone talking at once.

All the women cooking.
All the men happily staying out of their way.

All the children clamoring to spend time
with my father, Grandpa Andrew.

He had a knack for storytelling,
sending the youngest ones shrieking

under a table when he turned into a troll,
puffing out his cheeks, hunching

his shoulders and deepening his voice.
And when he took out one of Grandma's

good shawls, covered his head and began
speaking in falsetto, even Mama's eyes lit up.

> *We want to be like you, Grandpa,*
> one of the children would say.

> *Make us a play,*
> piped up another.

Papa never said "no," and I could always tell
by the way the years fell from his body

as he worked with the children to turn his story
into their play, that he enjoyed it as much as they did.

It was like setting a whirlwind loose in the house—
Papa speaking Swedish, the young ones, English;

children running around looking for props and costumes;
Florence and Elof practicing music for the production.

But when it was all over, when their make-shift curtain
came down after their performance, we'd jump

to our feet, hooting and hollering, proud of our kids,
grateful for Papa's patience in making them shine.

By this time, he and Mama had sold
their boarding house, moved

into a much smaller house across the street.
Papa had a garden and chickens to tend.

Mama had flowers.
Everywhere.

In her yard. On her windowsills.
By her kitchen sink.

Her favorites—fuchsia, oleander and myrtle—
spilling out of tubs on her porch.

All of them carefully tended.
Each one, a confidant.

When Papa died on February 18, 1910,
when Mama felt herself isolated

from conversations that more and more
were spoken in a language

she'd never mastered,
when the women in Alexandria,

women she'd leaned on began to pass on,
Mama descended into a loneliness

not even her flowers could fill.
Her youngest brother, Henry, once said,

Johanna was born
with tears in her eyes.

Only two when her mother died, not much
older than that when her father remarried,

still a young girl when he moved
his family to town and she took over

running the family farm with her uncle,
Mama grew up somber and serious,

weighed down by loss and responsibility.
She tried erasing the gloom

with tonics and elixirs.
Her flowers helped some.

Her grandchildren helped more.
But after Papa died, we knew that death

was the only thing
that would dry her tears.

Lighting Up the Prairie

We called my brother Edward "Lighthouse" Peterson,
because he and his wife Annie kept a light

burning in their window for anyone
needing shelter during a storm.

Even in fine weather, their home
was a gathering place for neighbors.

Conversation was good.
Annie's coffee was even better.

Edward and I had always been close.
The youngest in our family, we stood up

for each other when our older siblings teased us,
listened to one another's jokes and stories

when no one else was interested.
We got into trouble more times

than I can count, but no matter what we did,
Edward always made sure I was safe.

Later when I married Elof, and Edward
proposed to Annie, the four of us

packed up our belongings and headed
north to Canada together.

Edward was a godsend, a fun-loving,
light-hearted brother who forever brightened

the dark corners of our lives.
Come to think of it, maybe

that's the real reason we took
to calling him "Lighthouse" Peterson.

A Smooth-turning Wheel

As we entered the second decade
of the new century, our seventh year in Canada,

the wheel of our lives
was turning right smoothly—

plowing and harrowing and sowing in spring,
tending to growing wheat in summer,

reaping in late summer, threshing in early fall,
moving wheat to market in late fall,

paying on loans for our equipment in early winter,
fixing farm machinery in late winter,

waiting through the thaw in early spring,
back to plowing and harrowing as the year turned.

But whether or not the wheel would run
smoothly was anybody's guess.

A farmer knows it's foolhardy to expect
one season to turn gently and predictably

into another in the Canadian Northwest.
All we could do was pray and try our best

to partner with forces that without warning
could wrench the wheel of our lives and livelihood

to a grinding halt,
destroy every last bit of grain

we had saved and scrimped
and suffered to plant.

But thank the Lord, the wheel was turning
smoothly with the seasons cooperating

with longer and longer times between
when our wheat was ripe in the summer

and before the first killing frost in the fall.
With the extra days, we increased our yield per acre.

With the extra money, we bought new, efficient
farm machinery, and our yield went up even more.

We borrowed a friend's steam engine
to drive our threshing machine,

put the time we saved to good use
plowing our land in the fall

so we could sow earlier in the spring.
Our yield soared.

We had other help.
Scientists developed wheat

that didn't take as long to ripen.
Wheat prices rose.

Our farm became profitable.
What a smooth running wheel it was!

Yet we were gamblers, gambling on the seasons,
keeping our fingers crossed the wheel

would keep running smoothly.
And just like a gambler loves the wager,

I guess we loved it too.
A Canadian journalist said it best:

> *The lure of the wheat*
> *is the world-old challenge*
>
> *of big hope and big risk*
> *to the world-old spirit of adventure.*

We had to be ready to lose everything.
But as the wheel kept spinning,

and we kept winning,
we couldn't help but think

we'd reached the future we'd set out for—
a good and prosperous future,

a future we'd carried
enough hope to find.

God Stood Weeping
at Our Side

Taking the Big Risk

It was an offer we couldn't refuse, an opportunity
we figured we'd regret if we turned it down.

Looking back on it . . .
but you can't go back.

What's done
is done.

It was the spring of 1912.
Wheat prices were high.

An investor—a land speculator—
offered to buy our farm, give us

good money for our land.
We'd been reading about opportunities

to homestead in eastern Montana,
and we were tempted.

If we had more land,
we could grow more wheat.

If we had more wheat to sell,
we could grow a better future.

We decided to take the money
and move back to America.

Remember, we were people
of "big hope" and "big risk."

The "spirit of adventure" ran
in our blood. So did iron.

Strengthening the Nation

We weren't just immigrating to Montana
to put money in our pockets, we were going

to collect on promises like the ones
that had drawn us to Canada a decade earlier.

> *Come where the soil is fertile,*
> *where yields are phenomenal.*

Sound familiar?

> *Don't worry about rainfall.*
> *There's plenty.*

> *But even if we get less than expected,*
> *dry land farming—cultivating crops*

> *by using practices that preserve*
> *as much moisture as possible—*

> *will help you transform semiarid land*
> *into the nation's granary.*

Sound too good to be true?

You'll have everything you need to build
a community—railroads, telephone service,

roads and bridges, schools,
trading places and churches.

And the winters, though
sometimes cold, are never severe.

We set great store in that last bit
of make-believe. Too bad

the promise of mild winters was as full
of hot air as all the rest.

We'd heard these promises before,
but now, the government and the railroads

were adding something new—an appeal
to play our part in breathing life into rural America.

President Theodore Roosevelt promoted the idea:

The welfare of the farmer is of vital consequence
to the welfare of the whole community.

The strengthening of country life, therefore,
is the strengthening of the whole nation.

It wasn't just promises of good land
and good crops that convinced us.

It was the notion we'd be modern farmers
using modern equipment and modern techniques,

and our modern work on the land, coupled
with our old-fashioned values,

would transform rural America,
strengthen all of America.

It was an opportunity to be part
of something larger than wheat farming,

an opportunity to be
of service to our country.

Many years later, we wondered
if there had been something else,

something even stronger than patriotism
beckoning us to leave everything

we had built and begin again.
Had we succumbed to greed?

Considering all that would happen,
we'd never tell ourselves it was.

That would have broken us
beyond redemption.

Risking Regret

Under the Enlarged Homestead Act of 1909,
we could claim three hundred and twenty acres

in eastern Montana—twice as much
land as we had in Canada.

> *We have to go,* I told Elof. *Remember*
> *that little girl flying down a dirt path*
>
> *on a plank behind a horse,*
> *yelling at you to give her the reins?*

Elof nodded.

> *Well, she's still here,* I said.
> *Maybe not as wild, and hopefully*
>
> *a whole lot wiser, but still itching*
> *to take hold of those reins.*

We weren't the only ones
who believed in taking risks.

Edward and Annie decided to go with us.
So did our good friend and preacher,

Olaf Sutherland, and his wife, Carrie,
along with his brother, Louis,

as well as Andrew and Annie Jern,
and Gust and Tillie Peterson.

All of us wanted a chance
at a prosperous life for our children.

Maybe I'd do well to remember that
when regret grabs my heart

like a terrier and refuses
to let go.

America! So Free!

To celebrate our decision to return to America,
Edward wrote a poem about a family

drawn to settle in Montana's eastern prairie.
Knowing my bigger-than-life, laughter-filled brother

would put together perfect words to lift us up
and send us merrily on our way,

we invited all our friends who were going
to Montana with us to come over

and listen to Edward present his poem.
What a performance he gave!

Besides being a singer, a composer and a violinist,
Edward was quite a storyteller with a voice

that cavorted up and down, loud to soft,
low to high, tickling our funny bones,

moving the men to slap their knees, the women
to hide their laughter behind their handkerchiefs.

Written to honor the German friends
we'd made in Midale, it began,

I comit cross from Germany
Mitt wife unt Kinter tree

Unt settle down in dis fair land
America, so free. . . .

So to Montana out ve came
To homestead mitt some land.

Ve broke some sod, unt planted again,
Unt vorked mitt veary hand.

Already we'd started to snicker,
not because we thought Edward

was poking fun at our immigrant neighbors—
he'd never do that, my brother was a kind

and godly man—but because in attempting
a German accent, he couldn't help himself

from chuckling at his own words.
And when he got to the part where life

becomes so difficult that his wife, Katarina,
suggests selling their farm,

Edward took on the wife's lines
and then his own with gusto:

Ve sell de farm, ve off to town
Ve sell de pigs unt cows

Unt buy a place unt settle down
Have rest within the house.

No vifery dear, another year.
Ve plow unt seed the land

Perhaps be paid in veldt unt cheer
A style so great unt grand.

I nudged Annie who was sitting next to me,
noticed she'd wrapped her arms

around her sides trying to contain herself
as her husband squealed into falsetto

for the wife's voice then switched
to *basso profondo* for the husband's.

Suddenly Edward stood up.
He'd reached the climax of his poem—

the family's discovery
of oil beneath their land.

Mine Got, dat gusser was so grand
Him came met Geldt so feel

Unt start me on mine feet again
Unt make me strong like steel. . . .

Already, yet, Katarina too
She smiles unt say to me

"So schmart und vise it was for you
Dat ve so rich could be."

Unt effer happy we vill live
Dem hard days past vill be.

Unt hope, unt joy, each other give.
America! So free!

Edward trumpeted his final words with such force
he could've tumbled the walls of Jericho.

Elof shouted as he gave Edward
an affectionate rap on the shoulder,

Well done! You said it just right—
"effer happy we vill live" in "America! So free!"

The Hardest Love

In May 1912, Elof and Edward,
Olaf Sutherland and his brother, Louis,

along with five other Midale friends set out
to look for land in Montana's eastern prairie.

Their visit to one county was covered
by a local newspaper:

> *The first of a series of parties who are coming*
> *to Custer County from Canada*
>
> *to look over our land has arrived.*
> *It is understood that they*
>
> *are dissatisfied with conditions*
> *in their own section,*
>
> *and that they are contemplating*
> *locating in Custer County.*

We weren't dissatisfied in Canada.
We simply thought we could grow

more wheat in eastern Montana.
We weren't the only ones.

Between 1900 and 1920,
her population grew from 93,000 to 314,000,

a land rush described
by the American geographer Isaiah Bowman:

> *There was a fair chance for everyone,*
> *and the whole of the grazing country*
>
> *seemed about to become*
> *a prosperous farming belt.*

But why did so many of us risk everything
for "a fair chance" at "prosperous farming"?

For the same reason Grandpa Elias moved
his entire family from Sweden

to the Minnesota prairie—love
for his children and his children's children;

a love that held fiercely,
without evidence or guarantee,

to the possibility that land
could give them a future.

Elof and his friends narrowed their search
to an area forty miles northwest of Miles City

between the Missouri, the Yellowstone
and the Musselshell rivers,

in what would become Garfield County in 1919.
Like the land we'd homesteaded in Saskatchewan,

it had once been land of the Assiniboine—
people of the northern Great Plains—

people who, like us, must also
have held a deep love for their children.

A love that latches onto the slimmest
of chances no matter how great

the uncertainty, no matter how heavy
the fear; a love that hardships

can make the hardest
to hold onto; a love

that has to be big enough
to hold hope.

Drying Mama's Eyes

Elof and I and the children
spent the winter of 1912

with Mama in Alexandria.
It was hard for her to get around,

and we wanted to be there to help out.
Florence was seven,

Reubin would turn five in February,
and Gordon was almost two.

With us were Edward and Annie
and their five children, ages one to eight.

It was a crowd at Mama's, and I knew
we tired her, but the tears in her eyes—

the ones always ready to escape—
didn't flow quite as freely

or as often with grandchildren
in her sights. And soon

she'd have another little one
to brighten her days.

I was pregnant. Our baby
would come sometime in June.

It would be a spring
of new beginnings.

The "Lighthouse" Dims

Late in April 1913, Elof and I,
along with Edward and Annie,

went to Miles City so Annie and I could see
the area where we'd be homesteading.

Always more sister than sister-in-law,
Annie was a gentle spirit,

kind and tender-hearted,
her loving nature, a salve

for my grief when
we lost our first son.

I'd loved her from the moment
Edward brought her home.

When she and I first saw the land where
our husbands had decided to plant

our futures, neither one us was much
impressed, but Annie reassured me,

This will be a good place for us, Gedia.
Remember what Edward said in his poem —

"Unt effer happy we vill live
Dem hard days past will be.

Unt hope, unt joy, each other give.
America! So free!"

We laughed, shaking our heads
at the memory of my brother's performance,

thankful for his good nature
and optimism.

But life teaches us to take
nothing for granted.

While we were in Miles City,
Annie took sick.

She died on May 3rd. Pneumonia.
She was only thirty.

Edward, the light-hearted man
who kept a light burning

in his window for lost travelers,
became more than a little lost himself.

His love for his children
kept his soul burning . . .

burning, but not near as bright.
He never remarried.

Words Fail

We were heartbroken,
but not deterred.

We couldn't be.
There was no turning back.

Our Canadian land had sold,
Montana was ahead, with all its promise:

> *"once-in-a-lifetime opportunity,"*
> *"ideal climate,"*

> *"sufficient rainfall,"*
> *"high wheat yields."*

It was the beginning of June 1913.
I was back in Alexandria, our child due any day.

Elof and Edward were still in Miles City
taking care of homesteading business.

A measles epidemic hit.
I tried.

I tried so hard
to save them.

First Waldo, Edward's three-year-old son,
died the afternoon of June 2nd.

Then Florence, our oldest,
who would've turned eight in the fall,

the apple of Elof's eye,
died the evening of June 4th.

Then Reubin, our next child,
five years old,

my affectionate little poet,
died the morning of June 5th.

Gordon, two and a half years old,
smart as a whip, wasn't expected to live.

Words are too small.

Five days later, on June 10th,
I gave birth to Ruby Hildegard.

Gordon lived.

Where would I find words
big enough to live on?

Grieving Never Goes Away

I will never get the images
out of my mind—

Bending over my desk, sobbing,
writing words to send for Elof and Edward,

> *Come home. Florence, Reubin*
> *and Waldo have gone home to God.*

Elof walking through our door,
terror and grief and guilt in his eyes,

horror and fatigue in mine.
We hardly recognized one another.

Me collapsing on the floor.
Elof rushing to catch me.

Elof running to Gordon, hanging on
for dear life, Gordon's and his own.

Edward, the shadow
of Annie's death in his eyes,

engulfing his four children,
his light all but extinguished.

The three of us standing
at the gravesites,

watching three little caskets
being lowered into the ground.

But images aren't the only things
buried inside me.

What has stayed
in my heart, what still

brings me to my knees,
is the sound of our grief.

In the evening after the funeral,
Elof, Edward and I took our wagon

to a lake outside of town.
There under heaven,

we wailed long into the night,
our sobs strong enough

to quake the land
we stood on, sway

the stars in the sky
and their reflection in the water.

Even the moon
shuddered with our pain.

Reaching out to God,
we grieved for our children.

But never once,
did we shake our fist at Him.

We knew he was with us,
weeping at our side.

Our Children's Deaths Tested Us

I couldn't breathe.
I had to breathe to get Ruby born.

We couldn't think.
We had to think so we could care for little, lost Gordon.

We couldn't eat.
We had to eat to survive.

I couldn't forgive Elof for not being with me.
I had to forgive Elof if I wanted us to go on.

We couldn't forgive ourselves.
We had to forgive ourselves or we'd have nothing left.

We couldn't forgive God.
We had to forgive God. He'd reunite us with our children.

We couldn't recover who we'd been.
We had to accept we never would.

A Blink in Time

If only time had a tear in it, a door
where I could go back and forth

between my old and my new life, a window
I could steal through, see my children again.

I didn't ask God to turn back the clock,
only to let me pass through a crack in time.

>   *I promise I'll come back,*
>   I prayed with my fingers crossed.

Day after day, we slogged through time
as if it were the gumbo our soil turned into

every spring, thick and soupy
with grief and unbelief.

Moving in slow motion.
Or not moving at all.

Days erased.
Endless days.

Sometimes I'd have a rare moment
of forgetting lasting not longer

than the blink of a butterfly's wings.
Then without warning,

a wave of sorrow
would wash over me.

If only I could've lived
in that blink.

Engraved on Our Days

When we'd lost Carl Emmanuel, our infant son,
two things carried us through our grief—

our friends and our faith.
This time, our friends were scattered,

some still in Midale, some already in Montana.
None of them were close.

Our faith would have to lift us up,
give us a way forward.

We engraved on Florence's stone:

   We Shall Meet Again.

On Reubin's:

   Not Lost But Gone Before.

Our belief in the hereafter.
It was the one thing we could hang on to.

It was important to both of us,
but especially to Elof.

Every evening he'd pull out his book
on Christ's second coming, read aloud

the Bible verse he'd marked,
the one that told him

our family would someday
be reunited:

> *For the Lord himself will come down*
> *from heaven, with a loud command,*
>
> *with the voice of the archangel*
> *and with the trumpet call of God,*
>
> *and the dead in Christ will rise first.*
> *After that, we who are still alive*
>
> *and are left will be caught up together*
> *with them in the clouds*
>
> *to meet the Lord in the air.*
> *And so we will be with the Lord forever.*

Night after darker night, Elof would look
at me and recite these verses.

Gedia, we will be with our family again, he'd say.
We will see our children once again.

I know, dear Elof. They're not lost.
Not ever.

Those were the words
we engraved on our days.

Shadow's Way

There was one member of the family
who couldn't wait for a heavenly reunion—

our cocker spaniel who had been with us since Midale.
Shadow, who was forever following Florence and Reubin,

constantly getting tangled in their feet, refused
to surrender them to God.

He wanted them to play ball, chase him, run their fingers
through his fur. Now. In this life. Not in the next.

Every morning, he'd slip out the door,
cross the railroad tracks behind our house

and head to the cemetery. In the afternoon,
when I'd go looking for him,

I'd find him there, lying between
the graves of his favorite playmates.

> *They're not here, Shadow,* I whispered.
> *You'll see them again,* I assured him.

His eyes told me he didn't believe me.

How could they be here one day
and gone the next?

It's God's way, I said.

He nuzzled the ground.

It's not my way, I could almost hear him say.

Sitting down beside him, I said,

Sometimes it's not my way either.

Leavening

Time kept spilling over.
It soaked into the ground.

Vanished.
Days disappeared.

Then weeks.
Then months.

We couldn't move.
We couldn't leave the place they'd died.

We needed more time.
We decided to stay in Alexandria

until the next spring, the spring of 1914,
try to make ourselves human again,

strong enough to start over
on new land.

It was hard.
It became harder still.

The fall of 1913 we received a letter edged in black—
the announcement Elof's mother had died in June.

We prayed the new year would turn toward life,
but on January 16th, Edward's oldest son, Clarence,

seven years old, died. Another epidemic.
Then on June 10th, just before we were to

make our way to our new homestead,
Mama died. Her tears had finally ended.

I could say she passed them on to me.
But I'd be lying.

To be sure, I'd cried.
But I wasn't made of tears.

I never would've made it through that year
if I'd been like Mama.

I had been iron-willed before all the dying.
I became even more so after all the burying.

But if I became harder, Elof softened.
And thank the Lord he did.

One of us had to teach our children
how to leaven strength with love.

Time

I hated time during those months of death,
on every anniversary of those deaths.

But it was time to begin again,
leave Alexandria.

Time to build a house,
break new ground, raise a family.

More than a decade had passed
since we'd set out for Canada.

Elof was forty-nine.
I was thirty-six.

It was time we got on,
appreciate the time we had left.

When Just Living
is a Miracle

Making a Home in This World

In late summer of 1914, we left Alexandria
and boarded a train bound for Miles City, Montana,

a good-size town planted at the meeting place
of the Tongue and Yellowstone Rivers,

an Indian-fighting town founded alongside
Fort Keogh after Custer's defeat in 1876,

a ranching town with cattle herders fattening
their stock on mixed prairie grasses,

a commercial hub-of-a-town with two railroads,
the Northern Pacific and the Milwaukee Road,

a grown-up town with stores and services,
grand buildings and good public schools,

a thriving town that would grow from more
than 4,000 in 1910 to almost 8,000 a decade later.

But we weren't going to live anywhere close
to that upstart Western town.

After loading up a wagon with supplies,
we set out for our homestead,

forty miles northwest,
outside a place called Rock Springs,

a town that wasn't any kind of a town,
just a spot on the prairie with a post office

and what you might call a general store
if you were being mighty generous.

Thank the Lord, Elof, Ruby, Gordon and I
would be there with Edward and his children.

Everyone
together.

Now.
In this world.

The Sound Grief Leaves Behind

We got our two-room house built,
put in fences before winter set in,

were ready to break sod in the spring.
A clock had started, pushing us

to make our way back to the living, but now,
behind its ticking, there was another sound.

A sad, soulful sound.
The sound of Elof's sorrow

seeping out of the wood
of his old violin.

He'd drawn the bow across
its strings so many times

since the death of our children,
the hymns he played,

the grief he poured into them
had been absorbed by its dark body.

The music stayed in the background
of our days for a long, long time.

Salvation in the Desert

With a half-section of land
one mile by a half mile,

three hundred and twenty acres
of gently rolling prairie land,

we had twice as much land as in Canada.
More land to farm. More land

to separate us from our neighbors.
Edward's homestead was five miles away;

the homesteads of Olaf Sutherland
and his brother, Louis, about a mile from us;

the land of another friend, Gust Peterson,
a little more than four miles away.

Knowing how quickly the isolation of prairie living
can steal a person's will, dry up one's spirit,

we wasted no time in pitching in to help organize
Rock Springs' first summer picnic.

As I whipped up an angel food cake
to take with us, I asked Elof

if he ever thought about
our first picnic in Midale.

Of course I do, Gedia. Being with our family
and friends saved us after the death of our son.

We were quiet as we remembered how their love
had made it possible for us to go on.

Elof, I know you've heard me
say this many times—

it's love that strikes water
from a rock in the desert.

He thought for a moment,
then took my hand.

I think it's a sign, Gedia.

What is, my dear?

We're making our home in a place
named after springs bubbling up

from a rock in the prairie.
It must be a sign

that the people we love
will save us once again.

Life's Burning Bushes

I sighed, leaned on my hoe
and wiped my forehead.

> *Elof, the Bible is right.*
> *"We labor and have no rest."*

He laughed.

> *Gedia, you've always said*
> *you were made for work.*

> *I am.*
> *Just not this much work.*

Taking off my garden hat, I sat down in the shade
of the barn, closed my eyes and saw

Gordon running up to Elof, throwing his arms
around his Papa after the toy glider

they'd made together sailed across the yard
and landed safely next to the well;

Ruby sitting in her wagon, yelling
at her Papa to pull her faster;

Elof and me looking at each other,
both of us remembering

how hard it had been for him
to slow me down;

Edward's children shouting "Aunt Gedia's coming"
with such love I had to struggle to hold back tears;

Elof encircling the shoulders of an ailing friend
while I held the hand of his worried wife,

all of us taking comfort in my husband's
prayers and presence.

There were so many moments
of tenderness and joy whose value

I recognized only in the remembering.
Much better to stop when I stumble

upon them, bend down,
take off my shoes

and step out
on holy ground.

Steel Strong

We sent word for the midwife,
hoping she'd make it

through the snow drifting over
the top of fence posts.

Frankly, I could have gotten along
without her, it's not like I hadn't delivered

many a little one, but I have to admit,
I liked having her help

bringing little Judith Elaine*
into the world on that ripping cold morning

of January 18, 1916.
Loving and needy, she bonded

with her Papa immediately.
For him, it was love at first sight.

For me, I could tell right from the start
she'd gotten my stubborn streak.

Over the years, there'd be plenty of times
we'd butt heads like two obstinate goats,

but when we calmed down,
our strong-willed natures

kept us from giving up
on ourselves and each other.

In spite of the fierceness that flared
during some of our tugs-of-war,

a love as strong as steel
was forged in those firings.

I wouldn't have lived nearly as long
as I have without it.

* Linda Whitesitt's mother.

The Wheel Turns

The first few years in Montana
were good ones.

Weather was our friend.
Our land—and it was *our* land

(we received the patent in April 1917)—
was yielding twenty-five bushels an acre.

The Great War had increased Europe's need
for wheat, and prices were soaring.

Our Governor told us it was our patriotic duty
to plant every available acre we had.

Then the rains stopped.

Drought hit northern Montana in May 1917.
In 1918, it spread to us.

With it came the grasshoppers.
We spread poison bran mash over our fields.

I drove the horses while Elof broadcast it
from the rear of the wagon.

It didn't stop them.

With the grasshoppers
came wireworms and cutworms.

We scattered chopped fruits
laced with arsenic.

It didn't slow them down.

With the lack of rain came temperatures
soaring over 100 degrees,

wind storms and prairie fires.
We watched our crops

turn brown and brittle, burn
and shrivel to the ground.

One day, my unbeatable Elof,
the man who had faltered

but never fallen, walked
into the middle of our field,

dropped to his knees
and sobbed.

   Heaven help us, I prayed.

Swelling the Breeze

Drought-stricken in eastern Montana,
trying to coax grain out of dust-dry ground—

is that how Elof pictured his life at fifty-two,
almost thirty years after leaving Sweden?

The question must have played
on his mind when he was awarded

his certificate of naturalization
on September 24, 1918, in Glendive

(the county seat of Dawson County
about seventy-five miles from Miles City),

for although he stood tall,
filling with pride as he pledged

his oath of allegiance,
I could tell by the way

he avoided looking at me
that he wasn't himself.

After the ceremony, without a word,
Elof strode onto the courthouse steps,

squinted in the sun as he looked
heavenward, and in his rich-as-sweet-cream

tenor voice, started to sing
"My Country, 'Tis of Thee."

At first passers-by just listened,
then as Elof encouraged them,

they began to sing along.
With every note, they sang

a little louder, moved a little closer
to one another.

After the last verse, Elof started
"America the Beautiful."

Looking at him, I saw his brow soften,
the worried look in his eyes

begin to disappear. And still,
he sang and sang.

And then, silence.
People held their breath,

not wanting to disturb the memory
of the music they had made together.

When they turned towards Elof,
it was to thank him

for helping them forget
the hardship of their days.

Later, as he and I walked down
the steps, he took my hand.

> *I'd lost Him, Gedia.*

> *Who, my dear?*

> *God.*

> *Have you found Him?*

> *I have, Gedia.*

> *Where was He?*

> *On the courthouse steps.*
> *Singing.*

Hanging On

On a cold day—February 2, 1919—
Gladys Elizabeth was born.

She was a cooing, gurgling baby,
sunny and enchanted with the world.

Just who we needed
after a devastating year.

We took her birth as a sign
1919 would be better.

But that summer,
the drought persisted.

We hung on.
Sometimes hanging on

is all the hoping
one can do.

Chasing Honey

We had come to Montana when it was wet.
Then the state's desert cycle returned.

It was a calamity for all of us "honyockers" —
homesteaders buzzing from one sweet opportunity

to another, getting stung when
life didn't work out our way.

This time "the sting" was worse
than any of us could have predicted.

Crop yields plummeted from twenty-five
to two-and-a-half bushels per acre.

What little wheat we could grow,
Europe didn't need (what with the end

of the Great War in November 1918),
and the bottom dropped out of the market.

Commodity prices crashed.
Farmland prices fell by fifty percent.

Twenty thousand mortgages were foreclosed.
Half of Montana farmers lost their land.

We had to borrow money
for the first time in our lives.

Just a few years back in 1914,
the year we came to Montana,

the Governor had told us
we were building

> . . . an empire which will rank among
> the really great achievements of mankind.

And the same year, these words, words dripping
with honey, appeared in the *Montana* magazine:

> *To those who wish to make a success*
> *of farming . . . there is no place*
>
> *on the continent today where the combination*
> *of high yields, excellent living conditions*
>
> *and an assured future is so striking in evidence;*
> *there is no place where failure is so remote.*

Maybe we should've known better,
but who can blame us

for buzzing into that honey-of-a-place
with every ounce of energy we had,

every resource we owned, confident
we would find ourselves a farm

that through hard work
and a little luck,

we could turn into a future
worth passing on to our children.

Doorway to a Different World

Watching many of our neighbors abandon
Montana, we wondered if we should leave,

but there was no place for us to go.
No money to take us anywhere.

We stayed.
So did Edward.

As the drought continued to wring
our land and our spirits dry,

we realized it wasn't a farm
that was going to give

our children a future,
it was a school.

So in that parched summer of 1919,
a carpenter by the name of Ike Sandbacken,

hired by Reverend Sutherland and his brother,
built a one-room school house

about a half-mile from our place.
With blackboards on two walls,

wooden desks lined up in rows,
the school was ready by fall.

Gordon, almost nine, and Ruby, six,
were among its first nine students.

A decade later, Gordon would teach
at the Sutherland School,

stand in front of the same desks,
which by then, had been scarred

with the absentminded scribbling
of students daydreaming their way

out of geography and history,
Shakespeare and math.

He'd wonder, as he had since he first
walked in those doors, how he and his sisters

would make their way out of the dirt
and dust of eastern Montana.

He'd taken to imagining the world beyond
the prairie, knowing that once there,

they'd look back at how
and where they were raised

and be mighty grateful
to the Sutherlands for opening

its door and their parents
for pushing them through it.

Footsteps at My Side

Bad times called for praying.
Together. In a church.

We didn't have one,
but we did have a school.

So every Sunday we folded ourselves
into our children's desks,

sat our youngest ones on the floor,
held our babies and prayed for reassurance,

not reassurance life would get better,
for after suffering one loss after another,

we knew losses were a way of life,
but for reassurance we weren't suffering alone.

There were two hymns we turned to
Sunday after Sunday for comfort,

hymns Elof choose from his book of sacred songs,
Men's Songs, a collection he cherished

because dear Florence had written his name
inside the front cover—*Papa Elof Johnson*,

in her best seven-year-old script.
I often caught Elof tracing the letters

she had formed,
as if by touching them,

he could feel again
the hand of his beloved daughter.

One hymn was a prayer:

> *In the hour when pain and anguish*
> *And the ills of life betide,*
>
> *Be my soul's sure rest and comfort,*
> *Lord, with me abide.*
>
> *Whatsoever be my portion,*
> *Savior, guard me, Savior, guide*
>
> *And whatever doth befall me,*
> *Lord, with me abide.*

The other hymn, a promise:

The Savior's voice is calling
In accents soft and low,

"Come weary, heavy-laden,
And peace your souls shall know,

And peace your souls shall know,
That earth can never give;

In me find peace and pardon
And grace by which to live."

In the hardship of the years to come,
the giver of grace never once left our side.

The Words He Chose to Love

Elof had always been moved by words—
hymns, poetry, Olaf's powerful sermons,

books about theology and philosophy.
When he'd come across passages that struck him

or get tugged by phrases that wouldn't let him go,
he'd call my name, insist I drop what I was doing,

listen to the words that had caught him.
They never failed to catch me as well,

or maybe, it was his voice that drew me in.
I often thought the sky agreed,

for I'd swear she moved closer
just so she could hear him.

He read his books until he knew them by heart,
then read our neighbors' books and borrowed

books and magazines from the public library
in Miles City. He couldn't wait to get his copy

of the *Svenska Amerikanska Posten* in the mail,
couldn't wait to show it to me

when it published a poem he'd written
in memory of his fourteen-year-old niece

who had been killed in a train accident.
Addressed to her, it begins:

> *Föfblif i ro, du dyra skatt,*
> *Det stormar blott på jorden.*
>
> *Men där hos Gud är ingen natt*
> *Och ingen sorg är vorden. . . .*
>
> *Där, uti himlens sälla land,*
> *Där vilja vi dig möta.*
>
> *(Stay calm, you precious treasure,*
> *It only storms on earth.*
>
> *With God, there is no night*
> *and no sorrow. . . .*
>
> *There, in the land of heaven,*
> *we want to meet you there.)*

Elof's words.
Measures of a man

who never doubted
how the words

he chose to love
gave birth to who he was

and the meaning he laid
on top of his world,

a man who never wavered
in his belief that

    In the beginning was the Word . . .

Lighting Our Way

"The terrible twenties"—
that's what they called the decade

following the onset of the ten-year drought
that devastated the Montana prairie.

They were bad years, unbearably bad,
but I can't call them "terrible."

We had a family, and our children
were growing, not dying.

My memories of those years
twinkle in my heart like the stars

God laid over our tired prairie,
so many stars I often wanted to reach up,

grab a handful and sprinkle them
around my children to keep them safe.

We had little light of our own.
No electricity.

Only three kerosene lamps,
which the children weren't allowed to light.

One day Elof and I went to get coal,
and it was long past dark when we got home.

All three girls—Ruby, Judith and Gladys—
were huddled together in one rocking chair.

Gordon, their big brother and protector,
was sitting on the floor at their feet.

We were so late.
They were so scared.

Sitting in the dark.
Alone.

We never did have electricity.
Or phones.

We had few roads,
and we never got the railroad

they were going to build
to connect us to Miles City.

It was more than fifty years since Mama and Papa
had come from Sweden to homestead in Minnesota,

and we were living the same hard life
they had moved to Alexandria to leave behind.

Not that we complained.
What would have been the use?

Elof and I had to get pleasure where we could find it,
and the shimmering shawl of stars

we stood under on clear nights satisfied
our hunger for delight.

If truth be told, that's the real reason
we were so late getting home.

We'd stopped to stare at the stars.

> *What are you thinking?*
> *I asked Elof.*

> *I'm asking God for the strength to make it*
> *through these days. And you?*

> *I'm listening to God tell me*
> *I've got strength enough for both of us.*

No Use in Grumbling

I was tough, always had been.
During harvest—when there was a harvest—

Elof drove the six horses that pushed (not pulled)
our header (a machine that cuts

the heads off wheat stalks), and I stood
in the wagon receiving the heads, using

a pitch fork to even out the load.
That way we could get as much cut wheat

as possible into the wagon, and
we wouldn't have to stop so often to empty it.

Then, with the help of our neighbors, we used a thresher
to separate the wheat kernels from the straw and chaff.

Finally, we gathered the clean kernels into burlap sacks.
It was weeks of back-breaking work,

and we still had other chores to do,
chores that weren't always routine.

Like the time I went to find out what was causing
the ruckus in our henhouse, and a weasel

grabbed hold of the toe of my right boot.
Thank goodness I was wearing

Elof's heavy work boots.
I didn't get hurt, but I can't say the same

for the thieving creature I kicked against the wall,
then impaled with my pitchfork.

I'm tempted to say it was all
in a day's work, but that minimizes

how hard we worked, how hard it was
to keep on working.

I remember the day I was standing outside
washing clothes on my washboard,

when suddenly,
I began to bleed.

A miscarriage.
I was almost forty-five.

There'd be no more babies.
But there'd always be work to do,

that day and every day after that.
There wasn't anything to say about it.

Grappling to survive
is a good antidote to grumbling.

A Lesson in Living

To help us make ends meet,
I took a job as a cook for local sheep herders

at shearing time and lambing season.
I might be gone for as long as three weeks,

but you'd think it was three months
by the way the children hooted and hollered,

ran up to hug me when the herder brought me home.
But it wasn't me they were glad to see,

it was what I had in the wagon with me—bum lambs—
lambs whose mother refused to care for or nurse.

Quick as they could, the children would fit
long nipples on bottles and feed the lambs,

then make a bed of hay in the manger
for them to sleep in at night.

On cold evenings, they'd fashion a little pen—
a small pile of hay surrounded by chairs—

in one corner of the kitchen
and bring the lambs inside.

As soon as we went to bed,
the bleating would start

and no one would get any sleep.
Elof lasted as long as he could,

but finally he'd get up, order
the lambs be taken back to the barn.

Our children learned a tough lesson
mothering those adopted lambs,

then watching as some were killed
by nature's hand or our own.

Of course, the deaths of the ones
they'd cared for broke their hearts,

but once they'd mended,
Gordon and the girls discovered

that living through their loss
had shored up the iron

that ran in their Swedish blood,
the iron they would need

to live in a world
that takes from all of us

who and what
we cannot live without.

Slipping on the Present

Many an evening I sat by the stove, my hands
busy at work carding the wool from our sheep

into padding for quilts or spinning it into yarn
for stockings, gloves and caps,

while the children did homework problems
or drew on a blackboard in the kitchen.

> *Mama, please don't make the stockings so*
> *scratchy,* they pleaded. *They're so heavy!*

> *All the better to keep you warm,*
> I answered.

I liked quilting the best, designing the pattern,
picking scraps of material out of my box of old clothes,

seeing how their colors and textures fit together.
Sometimes I got lost in thought.

> *I wore this when . . .*
> *The last time Florence wore this was . . .*

Rummaging around the remnants of worn-out shirts
and dresses, time became slippery

as if every event I remembered, every feeling
I experienced, was happening now.

> *I am still that young woman,*
> I told myself.

Then with the next fragment,
time slid apart.

> *Who was that young woman?*
> *I wonder where she's gone.*

I wanted to go back, make the dress whole,
slip into it, live those years over again.

Make different choices.
See my lost children again.

Then I'd hear Gordon tease Judith,
or Ruby start a spat with Gladys,

and time would pull me back into the present.
Stuffing the memories inside the box, I'd ask,

> *Who's ready for a piece*
> *of my angel food cake?*

> *I'll cut it,*
> Gordon hollered.

You won't cut it evenly,
Judith complained.

Then Ruby would jump up to get plates,
Gladys go to the drawer for forks.

The here and now.
It's all any of us can wear.

A Smörgåsbord of Memories

When our babies were infants,
I carried them with me when I did my chores

or worked in the fields with Elof.
Once I almost lost little Gladys.

I'd put her down in the shade of a haystack,
turned to help Elof, when a sudden gust of wind

blew the stack onto our baby girl.
She didn't get hurt, but it startled both of us.

When the girls got a bit older, Gordon looked after
his younger sisters in-between teasing them

and persuading them to get into mischief.
All of them were drawn to the creek,

but knew they weren't supposed to go in it
unless Elof or I were with them.

But time and again, as soon as they saw me
disappear over the hill to round up the cows,

they'd head for the water, mindless
of my worry one of them might drown.

Without store-bought games to play with,
they were masters of invention—

turning kitchen chairs into sleds,
and their favorite, transforming the lid

of my gallon syrup pail into a rocket ship.
It must've been Gordon, our budding engineer,

who came up with the idea of putting water
into my pot, heating it on the stove

till the pressure built up and the lid
popped off like a rocket

and sailed into the ceiling.
Don't know how many times

I had to hammer the lid to get it to settle
straight on my pot again.

Of course they had chores to do—
feed the chickens and gather eggs,

help me collect and milk the cows,
empty ashes from the wood and coal stove,

hang up wash on the clothesline,
fill mattress ticks with straw in the fall.

The "chores" they liked best
had to do with food—

licking the cream that escaped
when they helped me churn butter,

using their fingers to clean cake frosting
from a bowl before they washed dishes,

stealing tastes of my chicken and dumplings
so they could delay setting the table,

sampling my version of root beer or soda pop
before taking a pitcher out to Elof in the fields,

eating the cantaloupes and watermelons
I asked them to pick,

then seeing how far
they could spit the seeds.

So many memories for this
old woman to feast upon,

I remind myself of my children,
hankering for just one more bite.

A Life of Taking Chances

It didn't take too many years of drought
for us to realize that no matter

how much the railroads and the government,
the scientists and the agriculturalists touted

the idea of dryland farming—the practice
of growing crops in a semiarid region without irrigation—

our land was never going to support
profitable wheat farming.

So in the mid-1920s, we decided to add cattle
and run both a farm and a ranch.

Turned out cattle weren't all that profitable either,
but it was another risk we had to take.

Every season we had to take a chance,
bet on the weather, guess how much wheat to sow.

To reap the advantages of wetter years, we had to wager
that any year might be wet and plant accordingly.

What if we put in too little
and had a good amount of rain?

That would be just as bad
as putting in a good amount

of wheat and having no rain.
We had to count on success.

Everything we did was staked on rainfall
that could vary as much as fifty percent from normal.

In years when our crop was running
eight to ten bushels per acre

(not terrible, but not the twenty-five bushels
we thought we would get when we moved

to Montana), we might make enough to pay
extra farm hands to help harvest

and market our wheat, but then we'd have nothing
left over for seed, taxes and interest on our loan.

In real bad years, when we cut what little wheat
we did have as hay for our cattle,

we'd sell off some of our herd in hopes we'd have money
for next year's crop, which also might amount to nothing.

Year after year, we laid down a wager on the side
of enough rain, a good harvest, high beef prices.

Then the rain wouldn't come,
and we'd lose more than we'd win.

But like any gambler,
we persevered.

We still had land, and who knows,
maybe next year, the rains might return.

No Amount of Hardship

Our children got mighty tired
of wearing hand-me-down clothes.

When Judith put on Gordon's
much-too-long-for-her bib overalls,

he'd grab the pants legs
and drag her around the kitchen floor,

him yelling, Judith screaming,
and me trying to referee

without interfering too much.
I wanted my girls to stand up

for themselves, become sassy,
stubborn and strong like their mother.

When it came to shoes for the children,
we'd order them from a catalogue,

but were never sure they'd fit.
If they were too big, I'd stuff

the toes with wool or rags.
If they were too small,

Elof would fill them with oats, add some water,
wait until the shoes stretched.

If they came with heels too high,
Elof would cut them down with a saw.

Did they ever make a fuss?
Of course they did.

All four left home as soon as they could,
never forgot how hard their growing years had been.

But for Judith, decades living in a city
made her nostalgic for prairie living:

>   *Kids living in the city don't know*
>   *all they are missing. As the saying goes,*
>
>   *"You can take the girl out of the country,*
>   *but you can't take the country out of the girl."*
>
>   *That's me! I wouldn't take anything*
>   *for my days growing up in the country.*

What was it in that dry, dusty, hard-to-make-a-living-in
country that couldn't be taken from my daughter?

I think it was the relationship she had with Elof,
the devotion that flowed between them.

It was the closeness she felt with Gordon,
Gladys and Ruby, connections that despite

all their teasing and rough-housing,
lasted till the end of their days.

And I'd like to think it was the love
we had for each other,

a love tested over time
and strengthened with forgiveness,

a love that no amount of hardship
could ever extinguish.

Flying Too Close to the Sun

One day, looking over the stubble in the field
left after harvesting, Elof said to me,

> *Gedia, we've gleaned our fields*
> *to the corners, left nothing*
>
> *for the stranger. I hope God*
> *understands we need it.*
>
> *I'm sure He does, Elof.*
> *We try to help when we can.*
>
> *Remember the family*
> *that showed up at our door?*

It was a cold winter night, a family of five—
mother, father and three children—

knocked on our door.
Hungry and tired, they'd abandoned

their farm and were heading west hoping
to find a job, but their car was running

out of gas, and they needed money.
We didn't have much,

but we did what we could.
I made them dinner, gave them our beds.

The next morning, Elof readied
our wagon (we didn't have a car),

and the family followed him
to Rock Springs.

There he filled up their gas tank
and prayed for their safe journey.

Another time we were working in our field
when a small plane landed almost on top of us.

The pilot was plumb tuckered out so we stopped
what we were doing, took him inside, fed him

and let him get some sleep.
Before he left, he asked

if Elof or I would like
a ride in his plane.

> *I'm as close to heaven as I ever*
> *want to get in this life,* Elof said.

> *No thank you, sir,* I told him.
> *I want my feet touching the earth.*

He took off, and we watched as he headed
southeast towards Miles City.

Elof, I hope he doesn't fly
too close to the sun.

I don't think his wings will melt, my dear.
That contraption looked pretty sturdy.

But Elof, he's so high. He looks as if
he could touch the clouds.

I paused for a moment, then added,

Do you think we flew too high?

Looking up at the plane that was vanishing
in the blue sky, he said,

Perhaps. But it wasn't pride
that carried us. It was hope.

Not even the hot prairie sun
can melt her wings.

Saving Graces

In the summer, sweat ran down my face faster
than I could wipe it away with my apron.

Days on end, temperatures climbed
over 100 degrees only to be broken up

by an afternoon in the mid-70s just to tease us.
In the winter, the cold froze my eyelashes

when I went to collect the cows, and the season
would last longer than our sanity could bear.

Storms were bad—thunderstorms that set
the prairie aflame, windstorms that tore

at our house and our barn, dust storms
that shrouded the sun, hail storms that flattened

our crops, stole our earnings right out of our pockets.
I remember when one storm with hail

as large as hen eggs beat down
our wheat all the way to the ground.

It had been a good growing season with the wheat
higher than we'd seen it for a long while, and

we were counting on a big harvest.
Nothing was left.

As Elof and I looked over our broken field,
I felt a tug on my apron.

>   *Hurry, Mama,* little Judith was saying,
>   *let's make ice cream before it melts.*

She looked up at Elof,

>   *Come on, Papa, you can help.*

Our children never knew
how many times they'd saved us.

A Life of Hard Stories

We had no radio, no newspaper,
nothing to connect us with the world

except letters from family,
an occasional visitor

or an infrequent trip to Miles City
where we'd pick up the news.

We heard that women won the right to vote—

    About time, I said,

found out about Prohibition—

    Don't approve of drinking, Elof muttered,

read that Lindbergh had crossed the Atlantic—

    Did the good Lord really want us to fly?
    I wondered,

knew Hoover was elected President—

    Hope he has plans to help farmers,
    we prayed.

But these stories took place
somewhere over the horizon,

and although we made note of them,
we had plenty to worry about

right in front of us.
Elof and I had made it through

one hard story after another,
survived a whole book of them.

Then in 1929, there was a story
we couldn't escape,

one that would erase
what little success we'd scraped

out of the land when rain
returned in the mid-twenties.

From Whence Cometh . . .

Crop prices plunged.
Beef prices plummeted.

What little we could grow
and raise, we couldn't sell.

Then in 1930, the drought returned,
and we had nothing to sell.

The weather was a constant trickster.
We'd look west, see dark clouds building up,

only to be overcome by a blinding dust storm.
After it passed, grit and dirt covered everything.

Sometimes the dark clouds came
with a sound like thunder, and we dreamed

rain was on its way.
But as they got closer,

we'd find ourselves surrounded
by swarms of grasshoppers

who ate the heads off
what little wheat we could grow,

who vied with livestock for fence posts
and the moisture locked inside.

They even sat on our pitchfork handles, eating
the traces of salt our hands left behind.

We'd reached bottom so many times,
but this time . . .

. . . Our Help

Thank the good Lord
for FDR and his New Deal.

Government relief checks
gave us a regular income.

The Public Works Administration
supported the construction

of Fort Peck Dam,
just north of us,

which gave jobs to our son, Gordon,
and many of our neighbors.

The best thing Roosevelt did—
he gave us back our hope.

Settling

When I look back on the 1930s,
I realize we were settlers

living an unsettled life.
Nothing was ever settled—

the weather, the yield per acre,
the price of grain and beef.

There were never any
signs of settlement—

no town grew, we'd had
too many downturns,

too many droughts,
too little we could depend on,

no railroad was constructed
to move our crops,

no electricity was put in
to light our way,

no telephone lines were laid
to connect us with each other,

no good roads were built
to get us somewhere.

Of course, we shouldn't have
expected to be settled.

The land we'd chosen and the weather
that moved over it would never allow it.

There was one thing we could do—
make our peace with being unsettled.

One day when that peace
was particularly difficult for me to find,

Elof reminded me
of Emerson's words:

> *People wish to be settled; only as far as they*
> *are unsettled is there any hope for them.*

I was never one for contradicting Elof,
but I couldn't help myself.

> *Elof, I don't think it would hurt us*
> *one little bit if our life was more settled.*

> *But then, my dear Gedia, we'd never find out*
> *who we are capable of being.*

Priceless

Grinning from ear to ear,
Elof welcomed twenty-seven friends

to our tiny house on November 1, 1935—
his seventieth birthday.

Although not one to hold much stock
in presents, he couldn't hide his pleasure

when he sat in the new rocking chair
the children and I gave him.

> *Now if I only had time to sit in it,*
> he laughed.

He reached over, squeezed my hand,
and I smiled at my big-hearted husband,

thankful for the tiny gestures of affection
he laced through my days.

Not that in public there was ever
anything more than a kiss

on my cheek, an arm around
my shoulder, an "I love you"

spoken quietly. But as fleeting
as these endearments were,

our children took note of them,
and all four grew up like their Papa,

devoted to offering those they loved
a love beyond measure.

Leaving the Prairie Behind

Although we had stitched old and new friends
into a community that sustained us,

the fabric kept tearing as drought and depression
forced our neighbors to leave their land,

look for lives in more settled places.
The friend we missed the most was Olaf Sutherland.

He'd been our preacher and closest
companion for nearly forty years.

From Alexandria to Midale to Rock Springs,
he had lifted us up with his words,

carried us back to the land of the living
after the deaths of our children.

Having none of their own,
Olaf and his wife, Carrie,

became second parents
to Gordon, Ruby, Judith and Gladys.

The threads tying our family together
were also unraveling,

not that we hadn't expected it,
not that we didn't want our children

to move on, make a life for themselves
somewhere other than the prairie.

Looking back, we didn't have them long,
only until they were old enough to move

to Miles City, work for their room and board
so they could attend Custer County High School.

It was hard for them, waking up in the wee hours
of the morning to make breakfast

for the family they were boarding with,
getting their charges dressed and ready for school,

going to school themselves,
preparing dinner when they got home,

doing laundry and ironing
in the evenings and on weekends.

It's a wonder they had time for their own studies.
But study they did, and they kept on studying.

Gordon, the inventor who was always puzzling out
how things worked, became an engineer and a professor.

Ruby, who cared for every
hurt creature she met, became a nurse.

Judith, always good with figures,
had a career as a clerk and a bookkeeper.

Gladys, who loved to keep the peace,
became a legal secretary.

None of them ever looked back.
Perhaps the rest, like Judith, were, at times,

nostalgic for the kinship that isolation
had kindled between them and the fun

they'd invented for themselves.
But there wasn't one of the four who felt

the least bit tied to prairie soil.
They couldn't wait to leave the dust

and drought of eastern Montana behind,
find their way into city living.

A Love Never
to be Undone

A Ritual That Sustained Us

The drought lasted until 1937, and by then,
we were ready to become, as Elof put it,

"retired farmers," move to Miles City, be close
to Judith and Gladys who had jobs in town.

Elof was seventy-two. I was fifty-nine.
The demands of keeping up our land

and our cattle had caught up with us.
When the rains returned, it was time to sell.

Living in Miles City with electricity,
a phone, an indoor toilet,

churches and stores, parades and picnics,
concerts and lectures, a movie theatre

and even a bowling alley,
took a lot of getting used to.

With fewer chores to do, our days expanded.
With houses close by, our world narrowed.

Our lives filled with friends, old and new.
There was a Baptist church we liked,

one that called us to work
on charity projects and mission programs.

Elof joined the men's group, spent hours
discussing history and theology.

I attended the women's circle,
made afghans for needy families.

In the midst of all that was new in our lives,
Elof continued to write in his journal

while I crotched, and just as he had done
so many evenings on the prairie,

he'd put down his pen,
lean over towards me and ask,

> How shall we respond
> to this world, my dear?

And just as I had always done,
I'd pick up our Bible with one hand,

put my other hand
on Elof's heart, and say,

> The only way we can,
> dear one.

Battle Weary

Tired and worn down.
That's how we look in a picture

taken of us in Miles City.
Are we really the same couple who,

forty years earlier as newlyweds,
had appeared so eager to step out

of the frame into the future?
Now with hair thinned and gray,

Elof & Gedia (c. 1940, Miles City, MT)

our bodies shorter and wider,
we look stuck, unable to move.

I'm in a pale, printed cotton housedress.
Elof's a bit more dressed up—

a buttoned shirt, vest and matching pants.
Was I getting ready to cook for company?

Was he anxious to sit down, talk about
the news with my brother Edward?

My hands are behind my back.
Elof's are in his pockets.

Are we refusing to give life more
than she'd already taken?

Elof's frowning, scowling, even.
Where is the young man who once stared

directly into the camera, dared it
to record his optimism and impatience?

My eyes are downcast as well.
What was it I didn't want

the camera to see?
Was it how tough

I'd had to become in order to bear
the hardness of my life?

Mind you, neither one of us ever complained.
When one puts on the pain of living

enough times, one gets used to it,
knows how to adjust to the holes,

put up with the scratchy places,
live with the welts and wounds that come,

all the while refusing
to call it suffering.

Yet wearing life's battles
had taken its toll,

and try as we might,
we couldn't keep the camera

from capturing the sorrows
that had weighed so heavy on our days.

Saving Grace

We lived in Miles City for six years,
years that saw our children leave home

to start jobs, and Gordon,
Ruby and Judith marry.

To send them on their way, I tatted
each one a lace tablecloth,

something delicate and beautiful
to remind them there was more to life

than hardship and struggle.
But by 1943, life was offering

little but fear and ugliness.
War was waging.

Judith's husband, Donald, was serving
with the Army Air Transport Command in Calcutta.

Gordon was working in Washington, D.C.,
caring for his ailing wife, Evelyn,

and raising their young son, Raymond.
They needed our help.

So Elof and I sold what little we had
and moved in with Gordon and his family.

Judith joined us to lend a hand
with Evelyn and little Raymond.

I don't know exactly how many miles we traveled
to get to our new home in Kensington, Maryland,

a little town north of Washington.
It must have been close to two thousand,

but I felt like we crossed centuries
and ended up in a new world.

We got to know our new home
by taking Raymond sightseeing—

the Smithsonian and Mount Vernon,
Arlington, the Lincoln and Jefferson Memorials,

the National Zoo and National Airport—
sights Elof and I thought

we'd never see, sights we knew
little Raymond would never forget.

We discovered a city full of history,
beautiful buildings and grand boulevards,

a city brimming with people we didn't know,
where noise and stifling humidity

hung heavy in the air,
a city where we couldn't find

our own history in the scenes
we saw around us

or in the good people we met at church.
We felt like strangers in a world

we didn't recognize, immigrants in a city
built on dreams not our own.

We missed Montana.

As hard as it had been on us,
it had mingled in our bones,

become a permanent part
of our body and our soul.

Torn from the history we shared
with the parched ground we worked,

the dust we breathed,
the endless sky we searched for rain,

we seemed different,
our hold on who we had been

threatening to slip
through our fingers.

Our saving grace was our family
and our love—

the love, stretched and tested,
broken and fixed,

that Elof and I had shared
through one tragedy after another.

I remember the words
from one of his love poems:

> Dearest, dearest sweetheart, my heart is full
> Of dearest love, God give us heavenly tides,
>
> That our little vessel smoothly lull,
> With you, forever, at my side.

Our sailing had been anything but smooth,
and the tides anything but heavenly,

but with God's help, we had faced
the storms together. And now,

in a strange new world, we were still,
gratefully, at each other's side.

Meeting God Halfway

For Christmas 1943, Judith and I
gave Elof a gramophone and a recording

of Beethoven's *Eroica Symphony*.
He was transported.

His fingers played along
with the music on the neck

of his old violin, his eyes focusing
on something far in the distance

as he hummed each theme.
One recording led to another.

Violin concertos.
Chamber music.

More symphonies.
Each one was his favorite.

> *Every note is a message from God*,
> he'd say to me.

Straining to take in the river of sound
that rushed passed him,

he felt his heart translating faster
than his mind could keep up.

Music had always been the way
Elof and God communicated.

Now at seventy-eight, when age and hard work
had stiffened his fingers, slowed down

his bow, crackled his singing voice,
when he could no longer

create melodies he felt
were worthy of God's attention,

listening to music allowed him
to meet God halfway,

rest in the place where
their conversation could continue.

Memories Only Two Can Read

While Elof listened to his recordings,
I planted a garden, looked after Raymond,

cooked meals for the family and helped
Judith with washing and ironing.

Elof always offered to give me a hand,
but after what I'd done on the prairie,

I could have done
my piddling amount of city chores

with one hand tied behind my back.
Yet, even with the ease

of city living, we kept busy.
We grew close friendships

with neighbors and church members,
sharing dinners at our house and theirs.

We watched after Skippy—
a dog we bought for Raymond—

who spent every evening lying at Elof's feet,
hoping the old man would take a break

from reading the newspaper,
bend down and stroke his fur.

Elof granted his wish—frequently.
I think it gave comfort to both of them.

When he wasn't reading the paper
or playing the gramophone,

Elof listened to the radio.
Both of us looked forward

to President Roosevelt's *Fireside Chats*,
the confidence coming through his voice

calmed our fears about the war
and our son-in-law overseas.

We had so many more things
than we'd ever had on the homestead,

even more than we'd had in Miles City,
things that made our work easier,

things that connected us
with the outside world.

But there was one thing missing,
one person missing—Edward, my brother.

I never got used to not seeing him,
laughing with him,

hearing him sing, sharing
chores at his house and ours.

Although he'd stayed on his homestead
when we moved to Miles City,

we'd still meet often.
I never knew Edward to turn down

my chicken and dumplings, and he and Elof
loved to make music together.

We were both as proud as we could be
when Edward won second place

in a state song competition
for his entry "Montana."

I can still remember
the final phrase from his refrain—

> My Montana! You'll never lag.
> You're the brightest star in our great flag.

Edward was certainly one
of the brightest stars in my life.

We wrote to each other often,
but it wasn't the same

as sitting across from him at the table,
watching him enjoy my cooking,

hearing his stories and his tall tales.
But even though there were thousands

of miles between us, I was comforted
knowing we were alive at the same time.

There was a force like gravity
holding us together, a connection

arising out of a history that went back
to when we were toddlers.

It was a bond built up
experience by experience

into a library of memories
only the two of us could read.

The Iron It Takes Two to Make

In November 1944, just as our lives
were beginning to fit into Washington,

Gordon got a job with Magnavox, a company
in Ft. Wayne, Indiana, that was making

radio systems for the war effort.
So Judith, Elof and I gathered boxes,

packed up the household and moved
with him and his family to Ft. Wayne.

By January 1945, Judith had a job
with the same company.

We had just started to settle in,
when on February 3,

Elof was admitted to St. Joseph Hospital.
Congestive heart failure.

I went to see him every day,
but the loneliness

240

of going home without him
weakened the iron

that had steeled me against
all the sorrows we'd faced together.

Last Entry

Wanting to hold in my hands
something Elof had held in his,

I opened his journal, strained
to read his last entry.

He'd started, as always, with words
about the weather—

Klart, fint (clear, fine)—
but then his hand had faltered,

and I couldn't make out the rest.
Picking up his pen, hoping

that by preserving his writing ritual,
I would bring him close,

I recorded those hard,
heartbreaking days:

> *Feb. 4. Papa at hospital. Felt good.*
> *Feb. 5 & 6. Still at hospital.*

Feb. 7. All lonesome.
Feb. 8. See him every day.

Feb. 9. He wanted
to come home.

Feb. 10. Dr. told me to advise the girls
to be ready to come home.

Feb. 11. Nice day.
Brought Papa home.

Walked to the house alone.
Glad to get home.

Feb. 12. Papa in bed.
Hard time breathing.

Feb. 13. Cardiac failure.
All worry.

Feb. 14. Wired the girls
to come.

Feb. 15. Gladys came home.
Papa glad to see her.

Feb. 16. Friday. Ruby comes.
Papa knows her and glad she is here.

But oh! passed away at 9 PM.
Everyone heartbroken.

My script is shaky.
My sentences are short.

My tears have
run the ink.

Turning Life Around

On Sunday morning, February 18, 1945,
Gordon, the girls and I, watched

as the coffin carrying Elof was put
aboard a train bound for Alexandria.

Taking our seats in one
of the front passenger cars,

I couldn't help but remember
how Elof and I had started our marriage

by packing our belongings
on a train headed for Canada,

how he'd held my hand as the prairie
passed before our eyes,

all the while talking about the homestead
our dreams were chasing.

Then later, lulled by the swaying motion
of the train, I closed my eyes and saw

another train ride, one that carried us
alongside the Yellowstone River into a prairie

of silvery sagebrush and rocky buttes
and a new beginning in Montana.

How different life looked now
as I rode the train back to the town

where we'd started both trips, wishing
that somehow the rails were moving me

into the past, giving me a chance
to live our lives over again.

Too Soon

While the children took care
of the arrangements for Elof's funeral,

I spent hours sitting at the front window
of my sister's parlor, looking out

at the town where Elof and I
had first met, seeing in my mind's eye

a young girl flying down a path
on a horse-drawn plank

while a handsome, young
gentleman held the reins.

It was yesterday.
It was a lifetime ago.

Picking up the memorial book
the funeral home had given us,

I added up the days God
had given my Elof and wrote:

After 79 years, 3 months, 15 days,
Papa passed away for a better home.

God might want him,
and I was grateful to have had Elof

for close to sixty years,
but I wasn't ready to let him go.

Words of Solace and Honor

Elof's funeral service was at
the First Swedish Baptist Church,

the same one he and I had attended
when we first met.

For one of the scripture readings,
I chose Genesis 25:8:

> *Then Abraham gave up the ghost,*
> *and died in a good old age,*
>
> *an old man, and full of years;*
> *and was gathered to his people.*

These words were for me.
I needed to hear that my Elof,

my old man "full of years,"
would be welcomed in heaven

by "his people" —
his father and mother,

our first son, Carl Emmanuel,
and our beloved Florence and Reubin.

At the graveside, I chose verses
from 1 Corinthians 15, ending with the words:

> *Therefore, my beloved brethren, be ye stedfast,*
> *unmoveable, always abounding in the work*
>
> *of the Lord, forasmuch as ye know*
> *that your labour is not in vain in the Lord.*

These words were for Elof.
Words to honor a man whose faith

never failed, whose hope never faded,
whose love never dimmed.

The Nature of a Man

Elof was surrounded by eighty family members
and friends at Engstrom's Funeral Home.

Their faces held admiration, love
and gratitude for having known Elof.

His sister Ella Erickson, who had emigrated
to Alexandria in 1888 (one year after Elof),

my brother Edward, and our old friend
Olaf Sutherland were there,

as were a number of his friends
from Midale and Rock Springs.

And there were friends he had known
from his first days in Alexandria,

friends like Anton Youngner who,
forty-eight years earlier, almost to the day,

had written in Elof's autograph book a stanza
from a popular poem and hymn:

251

Strange we never prize the music
Till the sweet-voiced bird has flown;

Strange that we should slight the violets
Till the lovely flowers are gone;

Strange that summer skies and sunshine
Never seem one half so fair

As when winter snowy's pinions
Shake their white down in the air.

Elof was never one to "slight the violets,"
take for granted what the good Lord laid at his feet.

All of Elof's friends had been drawn
to this quality—his ability to be rooted

in the day, take with evenness of temper
whatever came his way, knowing

the response was his alone.
They took to him because of his good nature,

his willingness to lend a hand.
They joined him on their knees

when he prayed for protection
and forgiveness, added their voices to his

when he sang praises to our Savior.
They were all a part of Elof's story,

thankful for having been written into
the life of such a gentle man.

Love That Lives On

At the funeral service, friends sang
two hymns he loved—

What a Friend We Have in Jesus and
I Come to the Garden Alone.

They filled the sanctuary with flowers.
Many of them made contributions

in Elof's memory to a children's home—
one of his favorite mission projects.

After the service, we shared
anecdotes about Elof.

One dear friend recalled
a time at her home just before

we left Miles City for Washington.
Everyone had been a bit melancholy

because of our impending move,
so after dessert, wanting

to comfort us, Elof rose to recite
one of his favorite Bible verses:

But as it is written, Eye hath not seen,
nor ear heard, neither have entered

into the heart of man, the things which God
hath prepared for them that love him.

Before sitting down,
he added,

> *Whatever the future holds, my friends,*
> *whether we find ourselves*
>
> *in this life or the next,*
> *God will be with us.*

That day God was with us,
in the affection that flowed

between Elof and every person there.
Remembering that day and the love

that surrounded us, God's and Elof's,
has kept my dear husband at my side.

Sustained by Grace

Back in Ft. Wayne, I opened
Elof's autograph book, hoping

his friends' words could fill
the empty rooms with his presence.

A small piece of paper fell out.
Unfolding it, I recognized Elof's hand,

saw it was dated just before we moved
to Ft. Wayne on the day he turned seventy-nine.

I'd see him look at the autographs
from time to time and smile

as he relived the memories
they brought to mind,

but he never mentioned
what he'd written on his birthday.

Now, as I touched each letter,
I felt him next to me.

Perhaps he knew I'd find his note
when I needed him the most.

November 1, 1944

Rereading these old and faded words,
my heart opens to a young man I find

difficult to remember.
I feel I should know the man

they address, and I can recall his face
in the company of his friends, but I find

it impossible to fit my seventy-nine years
into his twenty-year-old body.

Who was he? The years have torn my life
into many lifetimes, and I can't put the pieces

back together. They no longer fit.
Although young Elof is a stranger to me,

the path he walked and the way
he walked it are not.

Although I struggled and stumbled,
I believe I stayed true to one friend's counsel:

> *Let the road be rough and dreary*
> *And its end far out of sight;*

> *Foot it bravely—strong or weary—*
> *Trust in God, and do the right.*

The road that Gedia and I walked was certainly
"rough and dreary," strewn with death

and disaster. But as littered with defeats as it was,
I do not look back on my life defeated.

Did my family and I have a hard life?
Yes.

Were there times almost impossible to endure?
Many.

Was I ever tempted to give up?
More than once.

I don't think I ever became the man
or had the life my friends wished for me.

And I never did find the "good fortune"
my friends said would accompany me.

What I did find was a life of love
and a God who sustained me.

I would have asked my family
and my friends for nothing more.

Gustaf Elof Johnson

Crossing the River

Somehow life continues
through losses, through defeats.

We wade through grief, feeling
we're certain to drown, holding our head

barely above water, trying to catch
a glimpse of the opposite shore.

I had been in grief's river often enough
to know I would be in it until I wasn't.

There was nothing I could do
to ford it quickly.

I would reach the dry bank
on the other side in river's time,

not mine.
In the meantime, I needed

to move my body.
Sweat.

Become exhausted.
Immerse myself in dirt.

Be useful.
So I helped Gordon dig

the foundation for his new house.
With a hand shovel.

It didn't get me through
the river any faster.

It didn't make it any easier nor did it
lessen the effort it took me to stay afloat.

But it did give me long, uninterrupted stretches
of time to keep company with my memories.

It was healing work
as only working the earth can be.

After I was done, after the foundation
had been poured, I sat on the slab

with our dog Skippy, staring out
into the Indiana country.

I knew I didn't like being alone,
but I also knew my life wasn't over.

I sat on that slab for a long, long while.
When I finally stood up,

my feet found sure footing
on the far side of the river.

Gedia with Skippy (c. 1945, Fort Wayne, IN)

What Death Steals

I might have made it across grief's river,
but I made it there alone,

and after sixty years with Elof,
after all that time experiencing life

through two minds and two hearts,
I felt cut in half, forced to live

in a world where something
essential was missing.

I had to learn how to breathe
in a place where there was no air.

I missed the man. I missed
the comfort I felt in his company.

I missed seeing my reflection in his eyes.
When I lost Elof, I lost his Gedia as well.

His death shattered our history.
Not that it ceased to exist.

Not that my memories had faded.
Not that I couldn't piece it together.

But without Elof, there was no one
with whom I could re-experience

the wholeness of our life together,
re-imagine how we might have made

different choices, remember how,
one tragedy after another, we had

patched ourselves whole.
All of those things were still in me,

they'd just lost the light
that made them real,

the light it took
two of us to make.

A Vow

What kept me going
after the death of my Elof?

I was needed.
Gordon needed me to stay

in Ft. Wayne to help him
care for Raymond,

and then after Gordon remarried,
Judith needed me to move in

with her and Donald to help raise
their daughter, Linda, while Judith worked.

So in 1951, I moved to Great Falls, Montana,
a prosperous wheat-growing town

about three hundred miles from Rock Springs.
Seeing the prairie again,

breathing in its big, broad, blue sky,
I felt my heart stretch,

become a vessel large enough
to bear my loneliness.

I had returned home.

Now I travel to see Edward in Miles City,
and sometimes I visit my children

who are scattered across the country,
but mostly I'm content to stay home,

watch over little Linda whose gentle
disposition reminds me so much of Elof.

Standing over her as she sleeps,
I feel him at my side keeping his promise.

Sensing his presence, I place
my hand over my heart and whisper,

> *Forever,*
> *my dear Elof.*

It's a vow both of us
intend to keep.

Dearest Linda

I think this is about all I have to say.
There are more stories, more memories

hidden in the attic of my mind,
more feelings flaring up,

unexpected, almost forgotten,
like a prairie rain storm.

But these are enough,
enough to tell you who we were

and the history you carry inside you,
enough to tell you who you are.

As I've pondered what to say and how to say it,
I've uncovered missing parts of myself,

found ways to accept old choices,
let go of old failures.

Remembering the events of my life,
putting them in order, has helped me

relive my time with Elof, made me feel
like I've had a reunion with everyone in my family.

Being with them once again
has brightened my days.

Playing out pictures from my past,
I've felt again how good it was to stand

under the prairie sky, set myself free
to soar like a hawk over land that,

tough as she was,
never felt like a stranger.

I've been reminded how
in the spaciousness of the prairie,

places—people—possibility—
can rest just out of sight

on the other side of the horizon—
invisible, unknowable.

Believing in what cannot be seen
helps me hold on when life is uncertain.

Trusting in what cannot be touched keeps me going
when what I'm walking towards remains hidden.

As you ponder these stories,
know you have my strength,

Elof's perseverance,
our blood filled with iron.

Take with you the love
we counted on to last forever,

our faith that God would never
leave us alone.

As my story weaves its way
through your days,

imagine yourself standing
on Montana's big, broad prairie.

Look to the far horizon,
feel how wide the sky is.

Then reach up and gather
as much hope as you can carry.

Epilogue

From the moment I was born in 1951, Grandma Gedia spoiled me. Not with things, but with attention. I had no siblings to play with, but I had her. We'd sit on our old, red and gray striped davenport for hours as she read to me, and I'd pretend to read to her. She'd put me on a high stool in the kitchen so I could sprinkle brown sugar on the rolled-out dough of her cinnamon rolls. Around the coffee table in the living room, we'd play with my ceramic giraffes. One day I dropped and broke the neck of the smallest one. She started to scold me, and then laughed, realizing we'd just experienced a small earthquake (we were living in San Francisco at the time).

Grandma went with us when we moved to Baltimore in March 1958, helped me get through a bout of measles. Knowing now the story of how she lost her two oldest children during a measles epidemic, it must have brought up heart-wrenching memories of their suffering and death. I never sensed anything except her patience and concern.

On July 4, 1958, as we were coming home from a neighborhood picnic, Grandma had a debilitating stroke. Mother insisted that her mama was not going to a nursing home and brought Grandma home, but the effort it took her to care for Gedia began to take a toll on Mom's own health. After three years, she did the only thing she could, move

Grandma to a nursing home, a pretty good one by the standards of the day, but still one holding smells of neglect and isolation that were overpowering. Mother visited her every day, no small feat given she didn't drive and had to take two buses to get there. When I wasn't in school, I went with her, helping her carry the clean clothes she washed for Grandma every evening.

Gradually the fight seeped out of Grandma, the effect of the stroke too much for her body and mind. It was devastating to watch. Gedia died on September 14, 1963. She was eighty-five. Mother took Grandma to Alexandria and buried her in Kinkaid Cemetery next to her beloved Elof.

In 1895 when she was seventeen, Grandma wrote in Grandpa's old autograph book,

> *Smoothly down life's ebbing tide,*
> *May our vessels safely glide,*
> *And may we anchor*
> *side-by-side in Heaven.*

Their life was never smooth, nor was it safe, but I know that both of them are grateful that the last part of Grandma's prayer was answered, and that "forever," as both of them used to promise each other, they rest anchored "side-by-side in Heaven."

Notes

I am indebted to Gedia's sister Minnie Christine Johnson for her stories about their parents' and grandparents' life in Sweden, the family's immigration to America and their pioneering experiences in Minnesota, which she described in *Mother's Story* (© 1983 Glen Johnson). Minnie's stories were the inspiration for many of Gedia's pre-Canada poems.

Conversations between Gedia and Elof were imagined by me as I felt my way into their lives. Most of the comments by Grandma's parents and siblings are based on those published in Minnie's story. All other quotations, except for Elof's 1944 letter (my invention), are from original sources.

Bible excerpts are from the King James Version.

My Swedish Roots

Information (birth and death dates, place of birth, name spelling) about Gedia's parents and grandparents are from Jim Peterson, ed., *Lives & Lineage: The Peterson and Lindholm Families—Desmer Wallace Peterson, Gladys A., Clarence G., Ruth A. "Della," and Waldo R. Peterson* (LuLu.com, 2014).

Preface

Frederick Buechner, *Secrets in the Dark: A Life in Sermons* (Harper San Francisco, 2006), 137.

Dearest Linda

"It is all a battle, life up there . . . "—Agnes C. Laut, "The Last Trek to the Last Frontier: The American Settler in the Canadian Northwest," *The Century Illustrated Monthly Magazine* 78 (May to October 1909): 106, accessed July 13, 2018, https://books.google.com/books?id=849HAQAAMAAJ&pg=PA99&lpg=PA99&dq=agnes+laut+the+last+trek+to+the+last+frontier+the+century+illustrated+monthly+magazine&source=bl&ots=syoXRdk2Gg&sig=EVjVRC5Uz_DlFuRwLrSvlcg5WeY&hl=en&sa=X&ved=0ahUKEwi-irDRvPXWAhUH4SYKHUoaCEkQ6AEILzAC#v=onepage&q=agnes%20laut%20the%20last%20trek%20to%20the%20last%20frontier%20the%20century%20illustrated%20monthly%20magazine&f=false.

An Act of Faith

The Homestead Act of 1862 made it possible for each person age 21 or older to file a patent for 160 acres. Elias figured that his extended family could claim six homesteads for a total of 960 acres.

Turning Fear into Mercy

Henrik's story is quoted in Minnie Christine Johnson's *Mother's Story*.

A Threadbare History

Daisy Ellen Hughes, *Builders of Pope County* (issued in connection with the homecoming, historical pageant and dedicatory ceremonies celebrating the completion of Pope County's new courthouse in Glenwood, Minnesota, June 19–20–21, 1930), copy obtained at the Pope County

Historical Society as well as accessed July 13, 2018, http://pope.mngenweb.net/downloads/Builders.pdf.

Wait Upon the Lord
"But they that wait upon the Lord . . . " Isaiah 40:31

Finding Solace for a Lost Soul
The description of Gedia's grandmother is from Minnie Christine Johnson's *Mother's Story*.

A Love Never Finished
"Light" by Francis William Bourdillon. In Gedia's copy of *The Best Loved Poems of the American People*, selected by Hazel Felleman (Garden City, NY: Garden City Books, 1936), 38, she has marked this poem with a tiny slip of brown paper.

The Counsel of Friends
The quote by the Lutheran pastor is from Minnie Christine Johnson's *Mother's Story*. The dated entries in Elof's autograph book range from 1889 to 1897, roughly his first decade in America. When the autograph includes a place name, most are either Alexandria or Geneva Woods (a short distance from Alexandria).

Finding Our Place
Elof and Gedia must have acquired other property in Midale because Clarence Erickson, the author of a short blurb on my grandparents, indicates "they lived on the NE 13-5-11; a group of trees still marks the site. They also farmed S.E. 24-5-11."—R.M. of Cymri Historical Book Society (Saskatchewan), *Plowshares to pumpjacks: R. M. of Cymri: Macoun, Midale, Halbrite, 1984* (Midale,

Saskatchewan: R. M. of Cymri Historical Book Society, c1984), 344, accessed March 28, 2018, http://w w w . o u r r o o t s . c a / t o c . a s p x ? id=6142&qryID=585f0c31-49e4-43b0-825e-535ba0206 144.

When Uncertainty Becomes Possibility

Peter Hultgren, *A Brief History of Midale and District, 1903–1953* [Midale, Sask.: s.n, 1953], 3, accessed July 13, 2018, peel.library.ualberta.ca/bibliography/7399/5.html.

Singing Our Way to the Promised Land

The founding meeting of the First Swedish Baptist Church of Midale took place on October 25, 1903. In 1907 the congregation bought land and worked together to erect a church. The building was dedicated on January 1, 1908.

Reunion

"The Everlasting Arms," Ida L. Reed (lyrics), William J. Kirkpatrick (music); No. 60 in Elof's copy of F. S. Shepard, ed. *Men's Songs, No. 1: A Collection of Sacred Songs for Male Voices* (Chicago, IL: George F. Rosche & Co., 1900).

A Smooth-turning Wheel

About the weather in the Canadian Northwest, Agnes C. Laut wrote: "[The seasons] jump from summer to winter, and winter to summer, with such violence that all Indian legends of the seasons represent them as wrestlers in battle."—"The Last Trek to the Last Frontier: The American Settler in the Canadian Northwest," *The Century Illustrated Monthly Magazine* 78 (May to October 1909): 106, accessed July 13, 2018, https://books.google.com/books?id=849HAQAAMAAJ&pg=PA99&lpg=PA99&dq=agnes+laut+

the+last+trek+to+the+last+frontier+the+century+illustrated+
monthly+magazine&source=bl&ots=syoXRdk2Gg&sig=EVjV
RC5Uz_DIFuRwLrSvIcg5WeY&hl=en&sa=X&ved=0ahUKEwi
-
irDRvPXWAhUH4SYKHUoaCEkQ6AEILzAC#v=onepage&q=
agnes%20laut%20the%20last%20trek%20to%20the%20la
st%20frontier%20the%20century%20illustrated%20monthl
y%20magazine&f=false.

Strengthening the Nation

The summary of promises is a compilation of propaganda found in a number of different sources, including *Montana Free Homestead Land* (pamphlet published by the Great Northern Railway, 1912), 4, accessed July 13, 2018, http://cdm16013.contentdm.oclc.org/cdm/ref/collection/p267301coll1/id/3353.

"The welfare of the farmer . . ."—President Theodore Roosevelt, Special Message to the Senate and House of Representatives, February 9, 1909 (accompanying the report of the Commission on Country Life), *The American Presidency Project* online, accessed July 13, 2018, http://www.presidency.ucsb.edu/ws/?pid=69656.

The idea that "It wasn't just good land and good crops . . . " was suggested in Douglas M. Edwards, "A New Opportunity for the 'Man with the Hoe': Rural Reform and the Marketing of Montana, 1909–1916," in *Moving Stories: Migration and the American West 1850–2000*, eds. Scott E. Casper and Lucinda M. Long (University of Nevada Press, 2001), 101–102, accessed July 13, 2018, https://books.google.com/books?id=2EOuavhD3PoC&pg=PA99&lpg=PA99&dq=A+New+Opportunity+for+the+'Man+with+the+Hoe':

+Rural+Reform+and+the+Marketing+of+Montana,+1909–
1 9 1 6 & s o u r c e = b l & o t s = - d x - -
OH7SI&sig=aYOV2sraFchxMGF5asdkpuT7KJY&hl=en&sa=
X&ved=0ahUKEwj82uq64JzcAhVQIKwKHTQUCUUQ6AEIJz
AA#v=onepage&q=A%20New%20Opportunity%20for%20t
he%20'Man%20with%20the%20Hoe'%3A%20Rural%20R
eform%20and%20the%20Marketing%20of%20Montana%
2C%201909–1916&f=false.

America! So Free!

I found a copy of Edward's poem among my mother's memorabilia and then later, heard a recording of him reciting his poem on the DVD that accompanies his grandson's book—Jim Peterson, ed., *Lives & Lineage: The Peterson and Lindholm Families—Desmer Wallace Peterson, Gladys A., Clarence G., Ruth A. "Della," and Waldo R. Peterson* (LuLu.com, 2014).

The Hardest Love

The newspaper article entitled "Looking Over Land" was published in the *Baker Sentinel* (Custer County), May 17, 1912.

The land rush numbers are from Rex C. Myers, "Homestead on the Range: The Emergence of Community in Eastern Montana, 1900–1925," *Great Plains Quarterly* 10 (Fall 1990): 219, accessed July 13, 2018, http://digitalcommons.unl.edu/cgi/viewcontent.cgi?article=1394&context=greatplainsquarterly.

"There was a fair chance . . . "—Isaiah Bowman, "Jordan Country," *Geographical Review* 21, no. 1 (January 1931): 31, http://www.jstor.org/stable/208946. The area where Bowman conducted his field study in the summer of 1930 was the county in east-central Montana where Elof and Gedia settled in 1914, an area that became Garfield County in 1919. He went there to study a place where pioneer-like conditions persisted well into the third decade of the century.

Engraved on Our Days

Elof's book was E[ric] Wingren's *Kristi Tillkommelse och De Yttersta Tingen* [The Coming of Christ and Eschatology] (Chicago, 1910). The Bible verse is 1 Thessalonians 4: 16–17.

Chasing Honey

"an empire which will rank . . . " as quoted in Edwards, "A New Opportunity for the 'Man with the Hoe'" in *Moving Stories,* 109.

"To those who wish to make a success . . . "— *Montana* (1914) as quoted in Edwards, "A New Opportunity for the 'Man with the Hoe'" in *Moving Stories,* 106.

Doorway to a Different World

Between 1919 and 1925, almost 70,000 people left Montana.

Footsteps at My Side

The prayer hymn—"Lord, With Me Abide," F. S. Shepard (lyrics), Louis D. Eichhorn (music); No. 32 in Gustaf Elof Johnson's copy of F. S. Shepard, ed., *Men's Songs, No. 1: A Collection of Sacred Songs for Male Voices* (Chicago, IL: George F. Rosche & Co., 1900).

The promise hymn—"The Savior's Voice," Scotch Air, arr. and lyrics by F. S. Shepard; No. 28 in *Men's Songs.*

The Words He Chose to Love

The clipping does not include the date of publication. Translation by author.

The complete verse is "In the beginning was the Word, and the Word was with God, and the Word was God." John 1:1.

Lighting Our Way

"The terrible twenties"—Derek Strahn, "Feast or Famine . . ." on the Historic Homesteads page at *Distinctly Montana* (4 April 2007), accessed July 13, 2018, http://www.distinctlymontana.com/montana-history/04/04/2007/frontier-homestead.

Settling

Essays and Lectures as quoted in "Emerson on Talent vs. Character, Our Resistance to Change, and the Key to True Personal Growth," Maria Popova, accessed May 29 2019, https://www.brainpickings.org/2015/01/26/emerson-circles/

Memories Only Two Can Read

"Montana," Words and Music by E.C. Peterson, arr. by Florence B. Price, 1928, reprinted in Jim Peterson, ed., *Lives & Lineage: The Peterson and Lindholm Families—Desmer Wallace Peterson, Gladys A., Clarence G., Ruth A. "Della," and Waldo R. Peterson* (LuLu.com, 2014): 79–80.

The Nature of a Man

"Strange we never prize the music . . . " "If We Knew" by May Riley Smith.

1 Corinthians 2:9.

Giving Thanks

As I reconstructed Gedia's memories of her life on the prairie, I discovered my grandparents' place in the currents that shaped America at the turn of the twentieth century. I no longer wonder why they, along with thousands of other pioneers, emigrated to the plains of the Canadian northwest, or why they moved to the empty prairie of eastern Montana. I've found out how they managed to keep going through the deaths and disasters that plagued their lives, how their devotion to each other, their strong faith and their indestructible will gave them the fortitude to get up each morning, work as hard as they could, then lay their heads on their pillows at night knowing they had done everything possible for their family. The rest, they must have told each other, was up to God.

I'd still like to sit down with them—I'll always have more questions—but in profound and life-filling ways, I feel like I have. In the preface to this book, I suggest that doing the research to write it, delving through family artifacts, history and stories, searching for morsels of information on the Internet and in libraries, has been akin to gleaning a field. I never could have predicted when I started just how many gleanings had been left in the field for me to find. In looking and relooking at historical studies, in Googling again and again the people and places and events in my ancestors' lives, in turning over memorabilia in my hands, in having conversations with distant family members and friends I've uncovered in my gleaning, I've come away filled to the brim with more nourishment than I ever could have imagined. I certainly couldn't have anticipated that starting with just a few photographs and keepsakes, knowing only scattered birth and death dates, I would uncover a ground rich with details and meaning.

In retrospect, I've come to realize that one reason I started to hunt and peck for information and images that would bring Gedia and Elof alive, was that I long for family. I am an only child. My mother and father died within two years of each other when I was in my early fifties. I long to recover a feeling of attachment with the people who gave me life, people who live in my bones and run in my blood. In some amazing way, my search for knowledge about my grandparents' lives, insight into their dreams and the words to tell their story has given me the connection I seek.

For all that I've been offered during this "gleaning," I give thanks.

I am grateful to Grandma Gedia whose love fed me as I started to grow, and whose strength and stamina will inspire me during the losses that will surely come my way. And I thank Grandpa Elof for giving me a deep-down, soul-filling kinship with music and the messages it conveys to my heart. To both of them, I send a prairie sky full of love for having a daughter, Judith, my mother, whose generosity of spirit, good humor and selfless attention to me filled my life with a love like no other. They taught her well, and through the writing of this book, they've shown me how I might come to bear the hole left in my heart by her passing.

All the stories about life on the Montana homestead are based on memories my mom shared with me, notes she jotted in her journal, and entries in diaries she kept when she was going to school in Miles City. She was a preserver of family keepsakes—Grandpa's shoebox of memorabilia, Grandma's sister's story of their mother, photographs, and Elof's love letters to Gedia. It is impossible for me to say how grateful I am for her safekeeping of our family history, and there are no words big enough to thank her for loving me so fiercely.

I must have been about eight when I accompanied my father to the Library of Congress. He was working on a genealogy of the Whitesitt side of our family, also farmers in Montana, but on the western side in the Bitterroot Valley. I didn't understand what he was working on, but I could tell that he was excited about what he was discovering, and I loved being in such a beautiful reading room. But most of all, I loved being his "helper." Thank you, Dad, for inspiring me to delve into our history; I promise to tackle your side of the family next. During his genealogy work, my father shared his passion for digging into our family's history with his sister's daughter, my cousin Donna, and I thank her for giving me advice on my own search.

I am indebted to two people I met totally by accident through my clicks on Google searches—Dennis Pluhar, son of Inez Pluhar, daughter of Axel and Elna Haglof who bought Gedia's and Elof's eastern Montana homestead in 1937, and Jim Peterson, grandson of Gedia's brother Edward. They were both deep veins of connection with my grandparents.

In August 2018, my husband Bennett, my cousin David Johnson (Gordon's son) and I took Dennis up on his invitation to visit the old homestead. As we bumped through the prairie in his truck, circumnavigating the entire half section where Gedia and Elof eked out a living, Dennis painted a vivid picture of what life would have been like for them and at the same time, shared with us his own love of the land. "Paradise," he called it. Were there times before the droughts and the Depression sucked the ranch dry that Grandma and Grandpa felt the same way?

Dennis invited Annalise Willson (sister of Inez) and her husband, Jim, to accompany us on the tour. We were so glad he did. Annalise recalled meeting me when I was a little girl, remembered my parents, and filled in some of the blanks about life on this edge of nowhere in eastern Montana. Jim, who has written about the families who homesteaded in the area, had a photo for me of Elof's and Gedia's original, two-room house, and a plat map showing where the Johnson half section was located. He shared many stories about the courageous people who had been drawn to this prairie, and behind his words and Annalise's memories, we could sense the same affection for this particular piece of broad sky and windswept earth that had enlivened Dennis's descriptions. I am immensely grateful to the three of them for drawing me closer to my grandparents.

My quest for connection was also immeasurably enriched by Jim Peterson's work of love—*Lives & Lineage: The Peterson and Lindholm Families—Desmer Wallace Peterson, Gladys A., Clarence G., Ruth A. "Della," and Waldo R. Peterson*. I can't thank him enough for his book, for answering my questions, for sharing photos of my grandparents with me and most of all, for encouraging my journey.

Through ancestry.com I reconnected with my cousin, Colleen, Gladys' oldest daughter. We'd lost touch with each other after our junior high school days, and it was lovely to hear her voice again, listen to her talk about her mother.

Throughout the process of writing this book, I've found inspiration from a writer and teacher without whom my words would never have made it onto these pages. Maureen Ryan Griffin was, and continues to be, a mentor, a lover of writing and its power to capture and bring to life this precious human experience. I discovered Maureen when I was just beginning to think about writing about Gedia and Elof. Participating in her writing classes, being inspired and expanded by her spot-on suggestions, soaking up her encouragement, I gradually made my way to Gedia's voice and the story she had to tell. For all of Maureen's help "spinning words into gold" (the title of her treasure-filled book on writing),[1] I hold my hand to my heart and say "thank you."

And to all the sparkling writers I have encountered in her writing classes, writers who ask me questions, offer me alternative words and phrases, prod me to clarify and listen more deeply for Gedia's voice, writers who frequently send me in a direction where unimagined discoveries flow into my writing . . . and my life . . . thank you. I would especially like to offer my gratitude to Dianne Mason for asking me to read excerpts of my book to her poetry group in a retirement community. Seeing the members excited to share their own stories about their family history reminded me how so many of us long for a connection to people whose memories are buried within us.

To my family and friends who read the manuscript, Ginger Bailey, Kate Green, Mary Anne O'Hara, Donna Herrington and Lauren Draper, whose suggestions helped me "tune-up" Gedia's voice and whose encouragement and comments made me doubly appreciative of my grandparents' life; to Carol Grajek and Nina Norrman for

---

[1] Maureen Ryan Griffin, *Spinning Words into Gold: A Hands-On Guide to the Craft of Writing* (Charlotte, NC: Main Street Publishing Company, 2006).

translating Elof's sister's "old-fashioned" Swedish; and to Edith Patton, for listening to parts of Gedia's tale and helping me, through her questions, move closer to my ancestors and their stories—I say "thank you" for traveling this road with me and lifting me up when I faltered.

I offer deep appreciation to all of the archives, universities, libraries, and historical societies who have put so much information and primary source material on the Internet. Speaking as someone who loved ruffling through card catalogues and smelling the pages of old books, I miss the touch and the aroma, but it is a dream come true to have so many stories at my fingertips. On several occasions I contacted archives and historical societies, and I found enthusiastic, dedicated researchers who left no stone unturned to supply me with information about Gedia, her family and the areas they settled. The discoveries sent to me by the Douglas County Historical Society in Alexandria, Minnesota, were particularly invaluable in helping me unearth details about my grandparents.

During the trip I made in the summer of 2018, before visiting the homestead in eastern Montana, I spent some time in Alexandria and Midale, Saskatchewan, standing on the ground where my ancestors had homesteaded and looking in historical societies and libraries for more information about their lives and the histories of the places they had called home. The staff and volunteers I met could not have been more helpful. They love digging around in old books and photographs just as much as I do. For their impassioned and insightful searches, I would like to thank the following: Kim Dillon, Barbara Grover (whose photo-filled history of Alexandria teams with visual treasures),[2] Taryn

---

[2] *Images of America: Alexandria* (Charleston, SC: Arcadia Publishing, 2013).

Nelson Flolid, Glenn Van Amber and Sheri Plato at the Douglas County Historical Society in Alexandria; Brent Gulsvig at the Pope County Historical Society in Glenwood, MN (who gave me an extra copy of *Builders of Pope County* that I had seen online as well as histories of the Norunga Church that my ancestors had helped found);[3] and Jean Nielsen at the Miles City Public Library. And to Betty Kramer, longtime resident of Midale and keeper of the Midale Museum, I offer my gratitude for the walk through the cemetery (and helping me find the grave of Gedia's and Elof's first son), the visit to the Baptist Church and its library, and the tour of the museum filled with historical treasures. I am also thankful to Betty for introducing me to Kaylene Scharnatta who gave me a copy of her wonderful history of Midale, *A Walk in the Past . . . Remembering Midale the Way It Was*[4] and told me to check out prairie-towns.com,[5] an invaluable source of old photographs of prairie towns in Western Canada.

---

[3] Daisy Ellen Hughes (issued in connection with the homecoming, historical pageant and dedicatory ceremonies celebrating the completion of Pope County's new courthouse in Glenwood, Minnesota, June 19–20–21, 1930), copy obtained at the Pope County Historical Society as well as accessed July 13, 2018, http://pope.mngenweb.net/downloads/Builders.pdf;
Seventy-fifth Anniversary, 1871-1946, History of the Norunga Lutheran Church, Lowry, Minnesota, Anton H. Chell, Pastor (Kensington, MN: n.p.); *Centennial Anniversary, 1871–1971, History of the Norunga Lutheran Church, Lowry, Minnesota*, Nathan Huang, Pastor (Kensington, MN: n.p).

[4](Publisher unknown, 2018).

[5] *Images of Prairie Towns,* accessed August 28, 2018, prairie-towns.com.

My story has been determined by the place I was born—Great Falls, a city near the center of Montana, a grain-growing region in the northern Great Plains. Although I didn't grow up there, I spent enough summers at the Whitesitt ranch in western Montana that I think of myself as a Montana woman, a woman after Gedia's own heart, a lover of wide-open spaces and uninterrupted skies. Like her, I feel most at home in broad valleys and open plains, places where I can expand my sense of what it means to be human, places that are big enough to fill me with hope. So on behalf of both of us, I say to Montana—for your spaciousness that has given us room to live with uncertainty and your legacy of homesteading courage that has emboldened us to live with hope—thank you.

And to all the prairies I visited during the summer of 2018, places I had imagined and written about, it was an extraordinary experience to have conjured you in my mind's eye—your broad, blue sky; the smell of your plowed fields; the prickly feel of your dry wind on my arms—and then stand on the exact spots that Gedia and Elof had farmed, knowing that somehow Gedia had led me to my descriptions of you.

Finally I am grateful beyond measure to my husband, Bennett. Like the Montana plains and her pioneers, he gives me endless room to discover who I am, word by word, page by page, and in his recovery from lung cancer, models for me the toughness it takes to persevere no matter how bleak the outlook. Writing these stories, I've come to recognize he has something of my grandfather in him—the musician who renders his art with soul-stretching clarity and the husband who signs every card to me with the word Elof used when closing his love letters to Gedia—"forever." So to you, Bennett, my love, I offer my own "forever."

Resources:
Finding Gedia's Story

In the spring of 2016 when I began looking for my Swedish ancestors, I had a plastic bin filled with my mother's keepsakes, her high school diary and composition books, a JCPenney shoebox of Elof's memorabilia, a few unmarked family photographs, and in an envelope labeled, in my Mom's hand, "Linda, you will want this"—Gedia's sister's narrative about their mother and the family's life in Sweden and America.[6] I also had a dresser drawer full of Grandma's crochet pieces, memories of my time with her when she took care of me after I was born, stories my mother told me about her experiences growing up on the homestead in eastern Montana, and the anecdotes Mom had started to write down in her journal shortly before she died.

And I had determination. I knew if I kept looking, I'd find Gedia and Elof. What I didn't know was how much information, material that included several personal stories about my grandparents, I'd find on the Internet. I was amazed at what appeared on the screen when I Googled and clicked, putting in search words in a variety of different

---

[6] Minnie Christine Johnson, *Mother's Story* (© 1983 Glen Johnson).

combinations, going back days and weeks later and looking again. I had started with a plastic bin of memorabilia. I ended up with a treasure chest of stories.

Some of my discoveries were serendipitous, so much so, I started thinking Gedia was guiding my clicks. I found her brother Edward's grandson Jim Peterson and his book on his grandparents' families purely by accident. Trying to clear up the death date of Edward's wife, Annie Peterson, I noticed a "Jim Peterson" listed with information about Annie's grave on the website *Find A Grave*. I contacted him, and he graciously sent me photographs, answered my questions and mailed me a copy of his book *Lives & Lineage*.[7] The book is a wealth of research findings and stories about his family—my family—and the DVD that accompanies it, with the voice and music of his grandfather, is a time machine right into the heart of the people who made me.

Then I made another coincidental discovery (I like to think of them as gifts from the universe). Trying to clarify the exact location of Gedia's and Elof's homestead outside of Rock Springs, Montana, I happened to notice in my search findings an obituary about a woman who had lived in Rock Springs—"In Memory of Inez Pluhar, Rock Springs, MT." The name wasn't familiar to me so I had no reason to click on it other than I thought it might tell me something about Rock Springs history. It did more than that, it connected me to my grandparents' history. In the third paragraph I read:

---

[7] Jim Peterson, ed. *Lives & Lineage: The Peterson and Lindholm Families—Desmer Wallace Peterson, Gladys A., Clarence G., Ruth A. "Della," and Waldo R. Peterson* (LuLu.com, 2014).

292

The first four years of her life were spent living on Frozen Dog Creek which is 12 miles north of Rock Springs, Montana. She lived there until the age of four, when they [Inez and her parents Axel and Elna Haglof] moved to the Elof Johnson place—only four miles north of Rock Springs on the U-All Road.[8]

Now I knew where Gedia's and Elof's homestead was located. But I found much more than that. In the list of her survivors, I noticed that one of Inez Pluhar's children, Dennis Pluhar, still resided in Rock Springs. I located his business phone number and called him. He couldn't have been more helpful and more friendly, inviting me to visit the homestead and offering to show me around the area. I took him up on his offer, and in the summer of 2018, my husband and I along with my cousin David, went to see the old homestead.

Almost everywhere I traveled on Google brought up interesting, and sometimes revelatory, results. In the next few pages, I describe some of them. This is not a comprehensive list, but only an accounting of some of the stops I made along the way. I offer them in the hopes that others looking to tell their family's story might be encouraged to peck around the Internet to see what they might discover. If it's anything like my own journey, it will be a reminder that we are all part of Frederick Buechner's "one vast story about being human."[9]

---

[8] Stevenson & Sons Funeral Home (Miles City, MT: April 2017), accessed July 13, 2018, http://stevensonfuneralhomes.com/obituaries/inez-pluhar-age-84-of-angela-mt/.

[9] *Secrets in the Dark: A Life in Sermons* (Harper San Francisco, 2006), 137.

***

Genealogy websites like *FamilySearch*,[10] *Ancestry*[11] and *The USGenWeb Project*[12] are vast repositories of information, not just for names and dates, but for all sorts of background material, historical contexts, town histories, institutional records, census data, emigration information, links to newspaper archives, and much, much more. For example, on *The USGenWeb Project* I found "A Brief History of Land Settlement in Minnesota," which gave me a comprehensive overview of early settlement in Minnesota, including a history of native Americans in the area.[13]

I uncovered fascinating tidbits about my grandparents and great grandparents in early local histories. For example, in *Builders of Pope County*,[14] I learned that Gedia's father, Andrew, was one of the early supervisors in Ben Wade Township, and I was thrilled to discover, on the website of

---

[10] Accessed July 13, 2018, familysearch.org.

[11] Accessed July 13, 2018, ancestry.com.

[12] Accessed July 13, 2018, usgenweb.com.

[13] The U.S. Department of the Interior, Bureau of Land Management, General Land Office, *Minnesota Pre-1908 Homestead & Cash Entry Patents* CD-ROM, accessed July 13, 2018, http://becker.mngenweb.net/land2.htm.

[14] Daisy Ellen Hughes (issued in connection with the homecoming, historical pageant and dedicatory ceremonies celebrating the completion of Pope County's new courthouse in Glenwood, Minnesota, June 19–20–21, 1930), copy obtained at the Pope County Historical Society as well as accessed July 13, 2018, http://pope.mngenweb.net/downloads/Builders.pdf.

the Montana Memory Project, first-hand accounts of Gedia's and Elof's homestead, their children, and the school they attended in *Garfield County: The Golden Years.*[15] I counted myself very lucky to find the story about Elof and Florence playing music over the first telephone lines in Midale in the descriptions of early settlers (several written by the son of Elof's cousin, Clarence Erickson) in *Plowshares to Pumpjacks* on the website *Our Roots: Canada's Local Histories Online.*[16] And in two publications written at the time of Midale's semi-centennial, I uncovered details of Elof's and Gedia's founding with their friends of the town's First Baptist Church.[17]

---

[15] Fern Schillreff and Jessie M. Shawver (1969), accessed July 13, 2018, http://mtmemory.org/cdm/compoundobject/collection/p15018coll43/id/21874/rec/7.

[16] R.M. of Cymri Historical Book Society (Saskatchewan), *Plowshares to pumpjacks: R. M. of Cymri: Macoun, Midale, Halbrite, 1984* (Midale, Saskatchewan: R. M. of Cymri Historical Book Society, c1984), accessed March 28, 2018, http://www.ourroots.ca/toc.aspx?id=6142&qryID=585f0c31-49e4-43b0-825e-535ba0206144.

[17] Peter Hultgren, *A Brief History of Midale and District, 1903–1953* [Midale, Sask.: s.n, 1953], accessed July 13, 2018, peel.library.ualberta.ca/bibliography/7399/5.html; and Peter Hultgren, *A Short History of First Baptist Church,* "published on the occasion of its jubilee and held in conjunction of the forty-sixth annual assembly of the Central Canada Baptist Conference, June 3–7, 1953. Midale, Saskatchewan, Canada" [Midale, Sask.?: s.n, 1953], accessed July 13, 2018, http://peel.library.ualberta.ca/bibliography/7400.html.

Fairly soon in my research I realized that I could get an inkling of what Gedia's and Elof's lives might have been like by reading about the experiences of people living at the same time and in the same communities. Reading their first-hand accounts, listening to their oral histories and seeing photographs of their work in the fields, the interior of their homes, the picnics they attended, the churches where they worshipped helped me imagine living in my grandparents' shoes.

Online archives like *Saskatchewan Settlement Experience*, part of the *Provincial Archives of Saskatchewan*, was a treasure trove of remarkable, comprehensive, personal stories and photographs covering every aspect of the pioneer experience in Saskatchewan.[18] I spent days poring over it, wishing every community had such an extensive collection devoted to the people who settled it. On the website *Archives West*, I uncovered story after story in oral histories about homesteading in eastern Montana in the early twentieth century, truly an amazing project— *Montana Historical Society's Montanans at Work Oral History Project, 1981–1986.*[19]

Finding photographs on websites of historical societies helped me imagine myself in the places my ancestors settled. *Daily Life for Pioneers 1890–1914* was a wonderful discovery, with links to photographs, letters and other primary source material related to prairie homesteaders in

---

[18] Accessed July 13, 2018, http://saskarchives.com/sasksettlement/display.php?cat=1890-1900&subcat=Introduction.

[19] Accessed July 14, 2018, http://archiveswest.orbiscascade.org/ark:/80444/xv35924.

western Canada at the turn of the century.[20] The independent website *Images of Prairie Towns* preserves a remarkable collection of images, mostly postcards, of western Canadian towns.[21] And the online *LakesnWoods: A Guide to Minnesota Communities'* page, "Alexandria Minnesota Gallery," has beautiful photographs of 1907 Alexandria.[22]

To put myself into Gedia's life, I needed to place her experiences and those of her family in context, understand the historical currents they were riding that might explain the reasons behind their moves to Canada and Montana. Helping me were turn-of-the-century studies recounting the history of Swedish Baptists in America[23] and Swedish-Americans in Minnesota[24] as well as a history of Douglas

---

[20] Critical Thinking Consortium, accessed July 14, 2018, https://tc2.ca/sourcedocs/uploads/history_docs/Immigration/ Daily-life-for-pioneers.pdf.

[21] Accessed August 28, 2018, prairie-towns.com.

[22] Accessed July 14, 2018, http://www.lakesnwoods.com/ AlexandriaGallery.htm.

[23] Capt. Gustavus W. Schroeder, *History of the Swedish Baptists in Sweden and America*, (Greater New York, pub. by author, 1898), accessed July 14, 2018, https://archive.org/ stream/historyofswedish00schr#page/n7/mode/2up.

[24] A. E. Strand's *A History of the Swedish-Americans of Minnesota*, Volumes I–II (Chicago: The Lewis Publishing Company, 1910), accessed July 14, 2018, https:// archive.org/details/historyofswedish01stra, https:// archive.org/details/historyofswedish02stra.

and Grant counties in Minnesota[25]—all sources I found on the *Internet Archive*.

There were other contemporaneous studies and documents that provided valuable insights into my grandparents' lives. Particularly helpful were Agnes C. Laut's "The Last Trek to the Last Frontier: The American Settler in the Canadian Northwest,"[26] the government and railroad propaganda pamphlets that influenced Gedia's and Elof's decision to immigrate to Canada and then back to the

---

[25] Constant Larson, *A History of Douglas and Grant Counties, Minnesota: Their People, Industries, and Institutions*, Volume I (Indianapolis: B. F. Bowen & Company, Inc., 1916), accessed July 14, 2018, https://archive.org/details/historyofdouglas01lars, https://archive.org/stream/historyofdouglas02lars#page/n5/mode/2up.

[26] *The Century Illustrated Monthly Magazine* 78 (May to October 1909): 99–111, accessed July 13, 2018, https://books.google.com/books?id=849HAQAAMAAJ&pg=PA99&lpg=PA99&dq=agnes+laut+the+last+trek+to+the+last+frontier+the+century+illustrated+monthly+magazine&source=bl&ots=syoXRdk2Gg&sig=EVjVRC5Uz_DIFuRwLrSvIcg5WeY&hl=en&sa=X&ved=0ahUKEwi-irDRvPXWAhUH4SYKHUoaCEkQ6AEILzAC#v=onepage&q=agnes%20laut%20the%20last%20trek%20to%20the%20last%20frontier%20the%20century%20illustrated%20monthly%20magazine&f=false.

United States,[27] and a comprehensive examination of homesteading in their particular area of eastern Montana by the American geographer Isaiah Bowman.[28]

Along the way, I turned to a number of more recent scholarly studies on a variety of subjects—migration to Saskatchewan,[29] the wheat boom in Canada at the turn of

---

[27] The Canadian Pacific Railway. *Western Canada, including Manitoba, Assiniboia, Alberta and Saskatchewan: How to get there, how to select land, how to begin, how to make money.* ([Montreal: Canadian Pacific Railway], 1890?), University of Alberta's Peel's Prairie Provinces website, accessed July 14, 2018, http://peel.library.ualberta.ca/bibliography/1867.html; the Montana Bureau of Agriculture, Labor and Industry, *Montana* (Helena: Independent Pub. Co., State Printers, 1909), Internet Archive website, accessed July 14, 2018, https://archive.org/details/montana00montrich; Great Northern Railway, *Montana Free Homestead Land (*1912), accessed July 14, 2018, http://cdm16013.contentdm.oclc.org/cdm/ref/collection/p267301coll1/id/3353; and *Eastern Montana* (Chicago: The Railway, 1913), Montana Memory Project website, accessed July 14, 2018, http://cdm16013.contentdm.oclc.org/cdm/ref/collection/p16013coll56/id/16.

[28] "Jordan Country," *Geographical Review* 21, no. 1 (January 1931): 22–55, http://www.jstor.org/stable/208946.

[29] Randy William Widds, "Saskatchewan Bound: Migration to a New Canadian Frontier," *Great Plains Quarterly* 12 (Fall 1992): 254–268, accessed July 11, 2018, https://digitalcommons.unl.edu/cgi/viewcontent.cgi?article=1648&context=greatplainsquarterly.

the century,[30] the marketing of Montana to potential homesteaders,[31] the growth of community in eastern Montana in the early decades of the twentieth century,[32] a

---

[30] Tony Ward, "The Origins of the Canadian Wheat Boom, 1880–1910," *The Canadian Journal of Economics / Revue Canadienne D'Economique* 27, no. 4 (1994): 865-83. doi:10.2307/136188.

[31] Douglas M. Edwards, "A New Opportunity for the 'Man with the Hoe': Rural Reform and the Marketing of Montana, 1909–1916," in *Moving Stories: Migration and the American West 1850–2000,* eds. Scott E. Casper and Lucinda M. Long (University of Nevada Press, 2001), 99–117, accessed July 13, 2018, https://books.google.com/books?id=2EOuavhD3PoC&pg=PA99&lpg=PA99&dq=A+New+Opportunity+for+the+'Man+with+the+Hoe':+Rural+Reform+and+the+Marketing+of+Montana,+1909–1916&source=bl&ots=-dx--OH7SI&sig=aYOV2sraFchxMGF5asdkpuT7KJY&hl=en&sa=X&ved=0ahUKEwj82uq64JzcAhVQIKwKHTQUCUUQ6AEIJzAA#v=onepage&q=A%20New%20Opportunity%20for%20the%20'Man%20with%20the%20Hoe'%3A%20Rural%20Reform%20and%20the%20Marketing%20of%20Montana%2C%201909–1916&f=false

[32] Rex C. Myers, "Homestead on the Range: The Emergence of Community in Eastern Montana, 1900–1925," *Great Plains Quarterly,* 10 (Fall 1990): 218–227, accessed July 13, 2018, http://digitalcommons.unl.edu/cgi/viewcontent.cgi?article=1394&context=greatplainsquarterly.

history of America's tall grass prairie,[33] and dry farming practices on the prairie.[34] All of these and more were invaluable in helping me picture Gedia's and Elof's pioneer experiences both in Saskatchewan and Montana.

Sometimes I just stumbled on helpful information I didn't know I was looking for, like the chapter on Native American history in Minnesota, "Early Native American Life in the MNRRA Corridor," that I unexpectedly found in a book on the *National Park Service* website.[35] Other times I knew exactly what I was seeking—information about growing wheat in the northern prairies at the turn of the century, for example—and happened upon the very helpful study by

---

[33] Daryl D. Smith, "America's Lost Landscape: The Tallgrass Prairie," *Proceedings of the Seventeenth North American Prairie Conference*, eds. Neil P. Bernstein and Laura J. Ostrander (July 16-20, 2000; pub. 2001): [15]–20, accessed July 14, 2018, http://digicoll.library.wisc.edu/cgi-bin/EcoNatRes/EcoNatRes-idx?type=article&did=EcoNatRes.NAPC17.DSmith&id=EcoNatRes.NAPC17&isize=M.

[34] Charles A. Dalich, "Dry Farming Promotion in Eastern Montana (1907–1916)" (master's thesis, University of Montana, 1968), accessed July 14, 2018, http://scholarworks.umt.edu/cgi/viewcontent.cgi?article=3133&context=etd.

[35] Drew M. Forsberg, in John O. Anfinson, *River of History: A Historic Resources Study of the Mississippi National River and Recreation Area* (St. Paul District: US Army Corps of Engineers, 2003), 39–51, accessed July 14, 2018, https://www.nps.gov/miss/learn/historyculture/historic_resources.htm.

Amy McInnis, "The Wheat That Won the West: The Impact of Marquis Wheat Development."[36]

To make my way into Gedia's and Elof's lives, I read books by contemporary authors who have captured the hardship and grit of the immigrant experience, books like Jonathan Raban's Bad Land: An American Romance[37] and Timothy Egan's The Worst Hard Time.[38] I dove into monographs on specific communities like Barbara Grover's Alexandria,[39] which provided me with much needed context. I even found travel books helpful, especially travel books like W. C. McRae's and Judy Jewell's Moon Montana, which gave information about the New Deal in Montana.[40]

For background on homesteading, land records, land patents, naturalization and cattle brand registrations, I turned to government records, archives and university websites as well as state and city historical society websites. Particularly helpful were "Feast or Famine . . ." on the Historic Homesteads page at Distinctly Montana,[41]

---

[36] Prepared for Winning the Prairie Gamble: The Saskatchewan Story (Exhibit, May 11, 2004), accessed July 14, 2018, https://www.wdm.ca/skteacherguide/WDMResearch/MarquisWheatPaper.pdf.

[37] (Picador, 1996).

[38] (First Mariner Books, 2006).

[39] (Arcadia Publishing, 2014).

[40] (Avalon Publishing, 2009).

[41] Derek Strahn (4 April 2007), accessed July 13, 2018, http://www.distinctlymontana.com/montana-history/04/04/2007/frontier-homestead.

Historic Farms Study of Minnesota Farms, 1820–1960,[42] and the history pages on MilesCity.com.[43] Articles on newspaper websites like Lorna Thackeray's "Dirt, despair not the only hallmarks of Dust Bowl Days"[44] and the same author's "Dreaming on the land"[45] on the *Billings Gazette* website provided me with rich insights into Gedia's and Elof's Montana prairie experiences. And yes, I even looked at *Wikipedia* and *WikiTree* entries for overviews, quick information, ideas, search words, references, and other historical viewpoints.

As I clicked on Google search results, I realized posts on blogs could be very helpful, blogs like the one I discovered on *Historical Fort Benton*, where I found Ken Robison's "Hope & Opportunity: Homesteading in Montana 1909–

---

[42] Susan Granger and Scott Kelly (Prepared for the Minnesota Dept. of Transportation, June 2005), accessed July 14, 2018, http://www.dot.state.mn.us/culturalresources/docs/crunit/vol1.pdf.

[43] Accessed July 14, 2018, http://milescity.com/history.

[44] (Dec. 28, 2003), accessed July 14, 2018, http://billingsgazette.com/news/state-and-regional/montana/dirt-despair-not-the-only-hallmarks-of-dust-bowl-days/article_edb5d836-2e01-5244-abbb-b0affdbce829.html.

[45] (May 15, 2005), accessed July 14, 2018, http://billingsgazette.com/news/state-and-regional/montana/dreaming-on-the-land/article_86e65bab-dc0c-5a44-a9d3-19fe8a256fa6.html.

1920,"[46] and the information-laden posts on Carroll Van West's blog *Revisiting Montana's Historical Landscape: 30 Years in the Big Sky Country*[47] related to Miles City history (all with wonderful photographs). Also helpful was a post on Lum Kleem's blog *Saskatchewan and Canadian history and genealogy* entitled "How did Saskatchewan Pioneers Homestead?"[48] and Robin W. L.'s history- and photograph-filled post "Tracing a Harvestor's Timeline."[49]

Through all my research I had to keep reminding myself that I was gathering information to help me see my ancestors' lives through Gedia's eyes. So during all my Googling and clicking, reading and re-reading, making lists of questions and searching for answers, I made time to listen for Grandma's voice, use my intuition and my

---

[46] September 10, 2007. This posting, published in the Fort Benton *River Press,* July 11, 2007, accompanied a Homestead Photography Exhibition at the entrance to the Museum of the Northern Great Plains during summer of 2007, accessed July 14, 2018, http://fortbenton.blogspot.com/2007/09/hope-opportunity-homesteading-in.html.

[47] "Miles City as a Two-Railroad Town," Dec. 29, 2014, "Miles City's Boom, 1907–1925," Dec. 30, 2014, and "Miles City: Bust and Recovery, 1925–1960," Dec. 30, 2014, accessed July 14, 2018, https://montanahistoriclandscape.com/?s=miles+city&submit=Search

[48] Nov. 2, 2012, accessed July 14, 2018, http://aumkleem.blogspot.com/2012/11/how-did-saskatchewan-pioneers-homestead.html.

[49] March 12, 2015, accessed July 14, 2018, https://kissmytractor.wordpress.com/2015/03/12/tracing-a-harvesters-timeline/.

imagination, my remembered sense of a strong connection to Gedia, and let her stories speak through me. As I opened each memory, unpacking them like the Russian dolls she and I played with when I was a child, I did, as she predicted I would, find myself "waiting inside."

About the Author

Dr. Linda Whitesitt is the author of *The Life and Music of George Antheil, 1900-1959* and a number of studies of women patrons of music in anthologies and journals. In addition to her scholarly works, she has written a novel about a Paleolithic woman's quest to awaken her clan to their kinship with creation, *The Summer of Our Awakening*; a how-to-book on arts education, *The ARTS Book: Designing Quality Arts Integration with Alignment, Rigor, Teamwork and Sustainability* (co-authored with Elda Franklin); and a book written with her husband, Bennett Lentczner, on his battle with lung cancer—*We're Surviving Cancer . . . Today*.

A graduate of the Peabody Conservatory of Music of the Johns Hopkins University (BM and MM) and the University of Maryland (PhD), Linda is a musicologist, violinist and music educator. She has performed in orchestras and chamber ensembles in Maryland, Virginia, West Virginia, North Carolina, South Carolina and Florida; taught undergraduate and graduate classes at Queens University (Charlotte), Winthrop University (Rock Hill, SC) and Radford University (VA); coordinated string education programs for the public schools in Miami Beach; and served as a middle school and high school orchestra director (Charlotte and Bethesda, MD). Before retiring to Charlotte with her husband in 2013, Linda was the Director of Research and Evaluation for RealVisions where she led the evaluations of federally funded arts integration and professional development projects. She has served as a member of a National Endowment for the Arts grant review panel and as an evaluator for Young Audiences, Inc. Currently, she is a violinist with the Union and Salisbury Symphony Orchestras.

Why Linda wrote *hope as wide as a prairie sky*:

When I take in the fact that I am almost as old now as Gedia was in this photo of the two of us, I yearn to see her again, take comfort in her sturdy arms and listen to her stories about how she and my grandfather Elof scratched out a life for themselves and their children on the dust-blown prairie. I wrote this book to feel closer to both of them, to take my place in a lineage of strong-willed, courageous, full-of-hope Swedish-American pioneers.

Gedia & Linda (1951, Great Falls, MT)

Share your own stories about the elders who have encouraged you and the ancestors whose stories have shaped your life on Linda's website: *www.treestories.net.*

You may contact Linda at *linda@realvisions.net.*

Made in the USA
Monee, IL
14 October 2022

15870285R00194